LEARNING CYRILLIC

LEARNING CYRILLIC

SELECTED STORIES

David Albahari

Translated from the Serbian by Ellen Elias-Bursać

DALKEY ARCHIVE PRESS
Champaign / London / Dublin

Copyright © 2012, David Albahari

LEARNING CYRILLIC, Selected Stories.

Translated from the Serbian by Ellen Elias Bursać.

First published by: Geopoetika Publishing, Belgrade 2012

This edition © 2014, Dalkey Archive Press

First edition, 2014

Library of Congress Cataloging-in-Publication Data

Albahari, David, 1948-
    [Short stories. Selections. English]
    Learning Cyrillic : selected stories / David Albahari ; translated from the Serbian by
    Ellen Elias-Bursac. -- First edition.

    pages cm
    ISBN 978-1-62897-090-6 (pbk. : alk. paper)
    1. Albahari, David, 1948---Translations into English. I. Elias-Bursac, Ellen, translator.
    II. Title.
    PG1419.1.L335A2 2014
    891.8'2354--dc23

                        2014018566

Partially funded by a grant by the Illinois Arts Council, a state agency

www.dalkeyarchive.com

Cover: design and composition by Mikhail Iliatov
Printed on permanent/durable acid-free paper

The stories in this collection have previously been published in the following books:
Pelerina i nove price (Narodna knjiga, Beograd, 1997): Lolita, Lolita; Squirrel, Peanuts, Hat; Fingernails, Mouse; Robins; By the Light of the Silvery Moon
Drugi jezik (Stubovi kulture, Beograd, 2003): Learning Cyrillic; Stamps; Hitler in Chicago; Shoulder
Senke (Stubovi kulture, Beograd, 2006): Fireflies; Shadows; Plums in Saskatchewan; Stamps; Calgary Real Estate; Distancing; A Story with No Way Out; The Pajamas; Holding Hands
Svake noći u drugom gradu (SKZ, Beograd, 2009): The Ski Jump at Lahti; The Basilica in Lyon; Head Weight; Munich Ghost; Tito in Zurich; Footsteps
Unpublished stories: On Earth; No, No, and No; Goldfish; The Scent of the Other Side.

CONTENTS

I

Lolita, Lolita 7
Fireflies 15
Squirrel, Peanut, Hat 19
Fingernails, Mouse 21
Robins 24
Shadows 28
Plums in Saskatchewan 36
Shoulder 43
By the Light of the Silvery Moon 48

II

Learning Cyrillic 53
The Ski Jump at Lahti 75
Stamps 80
Hitler in Chicago 85
The Basilica in Lyon 89
Head Weight 103
On Earth 113
Munich Ghosts 120
Tito in Zurich 130

III

Holding Hands 136
Footsteps 141
Calgary Real Estate 150
Distancing 155
A Story with No Way Out 160
No, No, and No 165
The Pajamas 171
Goldfish 176
The Scent of the Other Side 180

LOLITA, LOLITA

I DREAMED last night of Lolita. As I spoke her name in my dream my tongue rose and fell obediently in a trip of three steps down a glowing arc in the dark hollow of my mouth. And not only my tongue, of course, for when I woke over on the edge of the bed, the comforter over my head, I could feel the pressure of an erection fade and my penis retreat, slowly, then quicker, as dreams always fade.

A little later, as my eyes became used to the daylight, I was no longer sure whether or not I had dreamed Lolita. Actually, even if I had, how could I be certain it was she? I couldn't recall a single description of her from Nabokov's book, and Sue Lyon, with those heart-shaped sunglasses from the Kubrick film, had never seemed to embody the true Lolita. Maybe, I thought, it was merely her presence that I'd dreamed? Maybe I was repeating her name because her body wasn't here in my dream and I was hovering over an empty place that needed filling? Maybe everything happened behind my back, and maybe the dream, as dreams often do, was toying cruelly with me and keeping me from turning around.

"Silly," said my wife, "to spend so much thought, so much spiritual energy on something that wasn't even real, something that never was real! How can a creature fashioned of words and sentences become a being of flesh and blood, even in a dream? Your dream is right: you did dream of the emptiness of words and you did wag your tongue, the only true part of speech."

We were eating breakfast, and crumbs of toast bounced off her lips.

I remembered a sentence from a friend's letter. "Interpretations of dreams," I said, "are boring. They only matter as images."

"Nonsense," said my wife. "Images are empty space that has been painted in: interpretations are the connective tissue, the glue. Without them the images burst like soap bubbles. Dreams are lost, my dear," she said, scooping mayonnaise from the jar with her knife, "but interpretations remain."

I didn't know how to respond. As of late, I am the one in our conversations who ends up with nothing to say, unlike before when she used to sit there, silent, while I spoke, wondering, at times, whether I would ever stop.

"Actually," said my wife, her mouth full, "the fact that you dreamed your dream here, in this country, in Canada, where the sexual abuse of children is the most heinous of all crimes, says more than your whole dream. And that is, you must admit," she said, sipping her coffee, "an interpretation, after all."

"If you mean to infer that interpretation matters more than art," I snapped, "we have nothing more to discuss."

"You writers are all the same," said my wife.

"Who is the same?" I barked. "Give me one example, one, just one."

My wife looked up.

"OK," she said. "Look, I know every man is an island, and among islands there are probably fewer similarities than there are among people, but please, spare me. All I am trying to say," she said, enunciating every syllable as if addressing a child, "is that you cannot separate the place from the dream, and you can never dream the same dream twice. What was water in one dream may be ice in the next."

She was right, at least as far as the ice went. The mercury in the thermometer had been showing a temperature, for days, of twenty degrees below zero, dropping another ten degrees at night. The house where we lived, mostly of wood, creaked and groaned, buffeted by gusts of wind. In the morning, in the back yard, squirrels tumbled into the newly fallen snow.

"No," I said. "That's not what I meant. It's not desire I'm talking about, or loneliness, it's helplessness. Actually, hope, submission." I did not, in fact, know what I was talking about, just as I didn't know why I'd dreamed Lolita. If it was Lolita.

"Sometimes, I think," my wife said, "all your stories about language and words are just ways of taking your revenge: you pile them up, arrange them, just to prove that despite the abundance they mean nothing, they are empty in a sea of emptiness."

"Is that why it wasn't Lolita that I dreamed," I asked, "but her absence?" I made no effort to mask my sarcastic tone.

"Interesting," said my wife, setting her cup down on the table, "even if you are being mean." On the rim of the cup gleamed a sickle-shaped mark from her light-red lipstick.

"If you were to remember where we began this conversation," she said, "you'd see that both of us have been saying the same thing, but maybe you can't, since a person who forgets dreams doesn't generally remember the words that came before them." She bit off another mouthful of toast, and two large crumbs, with an almost audible crack, dropped to my sleeve.

If before I felt fury, or at least irritation, now I registered a sense of serenity. It spread through my limbs with a gentle tingling all the way to my ears and toes. I remembered having a similar sensation a few days before in the evening, or rather late that night while I lay in total darkness, waiting for my wife to come home from seeing friends. The light of the street lamp colored yellow the snow that had just begun to fall, in golden clusters, filling the space, eradicating all else. The gentle tingling I felt then I had attributed to exhaustion, grogginess, a dull suspicion, but now I knew this had been serenity, submission, tantamount to self-annihilation.

I came here to disappear, I thought, to be one of those golden clusters. And the tingling stopped, or, more precisely, all the points joined and then parted again outside the window, above the city, over the river. I wafted like a thousand flakes, like a papery body of frozen water droplets, each distinct, uniquely perfect in its beauty and symmetry. Now, at the breakfast table, I could no longer hope for snowflakes or celestial heights; I could at best become the mound of bread crumbs reflected on the smooth table surface.

My wife reached over and rested her hand on my arm.

"Don't take it personally," she counseled me. "It isn't, after all, your fabrication. Every writer must wonder about his words, their emptiness, but in the end he has to replace the void with a fullness or the writing would be pointless. With you an even greater empti-ness is what follows the emptiness, like an endless chain of yawning openings, as if you are trading writing, or the story itself, for an infinite fall."

"Like a dream," I said, "where you keep falling and never hit bottom."

"Yes," she said.

"Or, as in a dream where you can't figure out what it is you're dreaming about."

My wife laughed aloud.

"You can't catch me with those tricks," she said, pressing my hand. "Let's go shopping," she added, "it will help keep you from thinking that everything is your failure." She got up, wiped her mouth, straightened her blouse. "Sometimes you've got to give yourself a break," she said in a firm voice, speaking to me again as if I were a child. "You can't spend your whole life trapped by constraints."

I agreed, but shopping was no help. I walked obediently behind my wife, pushing the large shopping cart into which she tossed things we needed, things we didn't need. As I surveyed the endless rows of bags, boxes and bottles, the overabundance, the sliced watermelons and chunks of cantaloupe, I felt a growing, almost tangible, nausea. In the vegetable department, where every ten minutes thin streams of water shot from little sprayers, I wetted my hands and splashed my face. When I walked back to the food aisles I was overwhelmed. Hundreds, thousands of words leaped out at me from every item, every can of fish or box of oatmeal, from the containers and plastic bags, and each of them, each word, carried within it the largest possible measure of meaning, an almost tangible weight. Each word claimed that only it was the real thing, that all others were illusions, phantoms vying to convince you to the contrary, of their fullness. My wife, I knew, would never accept such an explanation, for she could not believe that words were anything but air itself, shaped into sounds somewhere in the throat and palate. In the time it would take me to convince her, an avalanche of words, like the kind that rumbles down the near-by Rocky Mountains, would engulf us both, or at least me, and who knows when they'd find me, crushed and perfectly preserved on the floor of the supermarket.

I stopped pushing the cart, waved to my wife who was bent over the frozen fish freezer, and went out into the mall. I found an unoccupied bench between two large, artificial tropical plants, and sat down. Here, in this artificial reality, I felt a little better, I thought, I could breathe more easily, my thighs no longer quivered, my heart had stopped pounding, my eyes weren't welling with tears. Sappy pop music emanated from the speakers, air freshener gushed out of the ventilation grids, a gadget at the entrance to the computer store rang in soft tones whenever anyone went in or out, there were bells jangling behind the corner, down a different walkway. If only I could live with sounds and smells, I mused, thinking with genuine fondness of the mole and the lady-bug.

"Without images," I said aloud. "Without words," I whispered.

I guess I must have dozed off, then, for when I next opened my eyes I was bent over, slumped to one side, mouth agape, head limp on my right shoulder, legs sprawled, and a little girl was standing there in front of me. I thought I must be dreaming and closed my eyes, then opened them again, but she hadn't budged. She stood stock still, staring at me.

I straightened up, pulled my legs together, wiped away the spittle that had pooled in the corner of my mouth. I looked first right, then left. Then I turned and looked behind me. But I didn't dare to look back at the little girl. The very thought that someone might wonder what an adult man, and a foreigner no less, was doing with this little girl, a minor, stirred in me the most terrible fears, but despite my discomfort I could not help noticing, out of the corner of my eye, her pursed lips, the smooth skin of her neck, a curl of hair peeking from her blond locks, a freckle on her left cheek.

"Go away," I said to her in my language. I spoke as if addressing my feet.

The little girl didn't budge.

I looked over toward the supermarket entrance: my wife might come upon me any moment now, pushing a shopping cart loaded with hundreds of food items. I didn't know what I wanted more: for her to appear, or for her not to appear, to find me with the little girl, or hasten the little girl's departure by showing up. Should I allow her to draw conclusions that would certainly be fatal for me, or should I tell the story to my own best advantage?

Then it occurred to me that the little girl might leave if I started speaking my language. Maybe she'd think, I thought, that I am a fool, an innocent fool who only existed as far as language allowed. I glanced at her, grinned, and recited: 'Al' je lep ovaj svet,' an old children's ditty by Jovo Zmaj. Instantly I regretted not choosing something loftier, maybe lines by Dučić or Šantić or Popa. One must never underestimate the ability of a child to comprehend art and the world.

The little girl said nothing. She didn't even blink. All she did was rub her lips together.

She might just as well have stabbed me in the heart with a knife.

"Go away," I said again in my own language. I thought I might burst into tears. I was sitting there, in the heart of western Canada, in the middle of this shopping mall, this temple of consumer culture, far from everything, far from my nonexistent country, far from myself, and a little girl who was ten or eleven years old was threatening, with a single gesture, or, in fact, without moving at all, to destroy everything that was left to me.

"Go away," I said, once more, this time in her language. "Go home," I gestured for her to leave.

A shadow flitted across her face which I couldn't read, but the little girl stayed put.

If she doesn't move soon, I thought, I will get up and push her away, all the way to the toy store. I could already see myself in tomorrow's headlines: Immigrant sexually harasses young girl! Country at war with others creates people at war with selves! Are we, too, victims of the war raging on the European continent?

The little girl turned, following the line of my gaze, and raised her hand in the air. Then she looked at me again, and even took a small, a very small, step in my direction, and said, "You are old, aren't you? Are you old?"

I hesitated. "Yes," I said, finally. "Yes."

The girl laughed and ran off. Actually she skipped off, lifting her feet up high and swinging her arms.

My wife arrived only a moment later. "You had company?" she asked.

I looked at the shopping cart. The words I had feared moments before no longer meant anything. I said nothing. I got up and started pushing the cart toward the walkway that led to the parking lot.

"Who was that?" asked my wife.

Sometimes she can really be relentless.

"A nightmare," I said.

My wife burst out laughing. By that time we were at the car, and she was laughing while I took out the groceries and loaded them into the trunk. She laughed so hard, in fact, that she had to lean on the car. She was laughing later, too, as we drove over the frozen parking lot, through the snowbound streets and back alleyways; she laughed while we were in the garage unloading the shopping bags and things, and on the porch, while she was scrambling to unlock the back door as fast as possible. She only stopped laughing when we got into the house, though she did burst into giggles in the middle of the afternoon down in the cellar while she was sorting colored laundry for the wash. Late that evening, while I was watching the late news, she slapped her thighs a couple of times, soundlessly, I admit, but I was certain it was leftover laughter. Sound isn't everything, just as words aren't everything.

That night I had a new dream about Lolita. Actually I dreamed the absence from the earlier dream. I dreamed emptiness, but I knew perfectly well whose emptiness it was, who could fill that emptiness. And then because of something that was happening behind my back which I could not see at all as I couldn't turn my head, the absence, her absence, began to dwindle, the emptiness began melting away, and suddenly, as dreams have a way of doing, I found myself somewhere where soon enough nothing would be left. If only I could manage to say a word, any word, I thought in my dream, everything would be different, but nothing came out of my throat, and the walls of emptiness (or were they the borders of absence?) moved in closer and closer, and I felt how, slowly, then faster and faster, I was going, going, gone.

Then the pressure of my wife's hand released me, the dream relinquished its hold, and the shapes of emptiness melted into the features of her face, nearly blurred in the pale light of dawn.

"You had the dream again?" she asked.

I nodded. Why explain?

"You gasped as if you were choking," my wife said.

I nodded again. All of it, after all, was wordless. My wife remembered how my earlier dream had ended, she lifted the comforter and tried to see to my crotch. Then she reached in, touched my limp penis, and clucked reproachfully.

I knew what that meant: I had let her down, she caught me in a lie. But I also knew that none of it was going to change. Then, or now, or ever.

So we lay there, silent, each of us on our own side of the bed, waiting for daybreak.

for Eva Cossee

WHEN SHE WAS a little girl, Eva loved catching fireflies. She would put them in a jar, and then, at night, with the covers pulled up over her head, she would watch how the points of light flew around their little universe. The fireflies flew into the glass, slid to the bottom of the jar, and Eva felt her eyelids grow heavy. At the last moment, before she drifted off to sleep, she would tuck the jar under her bed, where it waited for her until the next evening. By then, most of the fireflies would have stopped moving, but she would have new ones in a matchbox that still held two matchsticks, and so the cosmos in the jar would come alive again. The flashes of light crumbled like stale bread, scattering every which way. That, wrote Eva in her diary, is kind of the way I imagine the world came into being: as a chaotic disintegration of light and dark. Several days later, she added, in pencil: without the jar, of course.

And then, one evening, the jar stayed up on the shelf, and the next morning, when she woke up, Eva wrote down, rubbing her sleepy eyes a few times: yesterday I grew up, and from now on I'm no longer a child. She tipped the fireflies out into the bushes, tossed the jar into the trash, along with the lid, though later it occurred to her that she ought to have saved it and used it for something else. Meanwhile the garbage collectors came by, so when Eva peered into the trash can, there was nothing in it. Too late, Eva thought. She felt a wave of sadness rise in her and for a moment she had to take hold of the edge of the trash can, sure that she'd fall.

She didn't fall. She kept growing. She had forgotten about the fireflies altogether, though she still liked there to be a light on at night in her bedroom, whether she was alone in the apartment, or there was someone else with her. When asked why, she would tell any number of stories about moments of fear, scary dreams that she had not, in fact, ever dreamed, about how her parents once, without meaning to, had left her alone at home, and about a winter night when a stranger pressed his face up against her window and stared at her for a long time, pressing his lips up against the windowpane. She wanted to scream, call for help, but fear clamped down on her throat and stole her voice, and all she could do was see how his warm breath condensed into droplets, and how the droplets froze into ice.

She thought of the fireflies again for the first time twelve years later. She was sitting on a bench in a park, waiting for a boy who was supposed to take her to the movies. The evening was descending across the sky like a dark sheet spread out from the wash. The boy was late, Eva could see he was when she turned and looked up at the clock on the City Hall, and then, as she moved to look back, she caught sight of a firefly. What she caught sight of, in fact, was the glow of its light, and then, several seconds later, the glow of another firefly, about three or four paces off. Then the first firefly glowed again, the second replied, and then a third chimed in with its glow, then a fourth and fifth, and soon two bushes and the grass around them were glimmering as if they were decked out for Christmas. Eva watched them until she felt her neck ache. She looked up at the clock and realized that the movie had started awhile ago. She did not, however, feel any anger. In fact, she told the girl she was sharing the apartment with, I was happy.

The girl laughed when she heard what had made Eva speak of happiness. Where she was from, the girl said, fireflies were practically pests. Before she came to the capital city to study at the university, there were so many fireflies where she used to live that sometimes you couldn't breathe. Whole fields, the girl said, flashed on and off at once, like some sort of blinking ad. Once, she added, she could see how several bushes were flashing in sequence, one after another, as if the light was moving from the closest bush to the furthest, and then returning, the way news travels when it is sent by smoke signals. When she was little, said the girl, all the children where she was from had boxes in their pockets full of fireflies, and then all the fireflies would vanish, and all of us knew, she said, that the summer was about to end. A stray firefly would survive in our boxes, she said, but their lights went out pretty soon, too, and when they were all gone, that was when school began. Another reason not to like them, said the girl and laughed again.

Eva laughed too, and then she remembered her jar. She remembered the moment when she went to the trash can, lifted the lid and tossed the empty jar into the trash, and then she remembered that other moment, when she had to hold on to the edge of the can so that she wouldn't fall. Strange, thought Eva, but we grieve the most profoundly for lost absence, for a space no longer inhabited by those we loved. Afterwards she straightened up and told the girl she shared the apartment with that it was all about those we thought we loved, because we can't love anyone really, except, of course, she said, ourselves. The girl didn't believe her, you could see that in her suspicious eyes and the shaking of her head. And besides, she had been with the same guy for six years, Eva concluded, so the world already must look to her like a thoroughly studied subject.

In that sense, Eva said to a couple of guys she met at a singles bar, I am an eternal repeater, I'm still in first grade. She laughed, banged her hands on the bar, the guys exchanged glances, turned around and left. I won't cry, thought Eva, but the tears were already dripping onto her napkin. She brushed them away with her arm, and only then, when she had caught sight of the splotches of color on her skin, did she remember the make-up she had put on a little over a half hour before she went to the bar, paying special attention to glitter on her temples and eyelids. It is not easy to be a firefly, she whispered to the napkin. Then her shoulders began to shake with sobs, and the barman had to call a cab to take her home. He gave her a sack of peanuts for the road, and while she licked the salt from the big nuts and stared at the shimmering neon lights, Eva promised herself that she would go back and start over. "I am turning a new page in my life," she told the cab driver. The cab driver said nothing. "I know you don't believe me," said Eva, "but you'll see I'm serious. Extremely serious," she added. The cab driver started whistling then, but Eva, no matter how hard she tried, couldn't remember the name of the song.

Many years later, perhaps it was spring, she remembered another song, but that was a song a different man was humming. They met at a bookstore. Eva was leafing through books about insects, and he, when he saw her studying pictures of bugs and butterflies, stopped humming and offered to help. He was an entymologist, he explained, and insects were, in fact, his life. "I am interested in fire-flies," said Eva. "Ah," said the man, "fireflies are wonderful, but they don't have an easy time of it, because there is one female for every fifty males." "Are you telling me," said Eva, "that they glow so that they'll find a female?" "Precisely," said the man, "first the male glows, flying low over the grass, then the female glows, who has no wings and is crouching on a grass blade or twig, and after six or seven exchanges of light signals like that, they start to mate, though some females, when the mating is done, devour their lover." "I didn't know that," said Eva. She felt sick to her stomach and her mouth twisted in disgust. The man smiled. "In the world of insects this often happens," he said, "but the mating doesn't stop, even if it means a loss of life." "There are things," Eva said, "I will never understand."

The next morning, after she had had her shower, she looked at the reflection of her body in the mirror. If I were a firefly, she won-dered, which part of my body would glow? She thought about a yel-lowgreenish glow in the stomach, then on the forehead and cheeks, and then finally decided on her breasts. She put a blouse on, but-toned it up, but the glow shone through the cloth, like little halos. At most, fireflies live a week, said the man, and during that time they do nothing but glow. Then he fell asleep. If I put something else on, Eva consoled herself, the glow will be hidden. She opened the closet, lifted her hand to touch the folded clothing. She thought at that mo-ment of the fireflies that never did find a female in that week, and then no matter how hard she tried, she couldn't remember what it was she was looking for.

MY FATHER never told me the story behind his old hat, dusky in color. I recently thought of that. I was sitting on the threshold feeding a squirrel a peanut. The squirrel stood on its hind legs, took the peanut with its front paws, turned its back to me and covered itself with its thick tail. The tail was dusky; that is why I thought of Father's old hat. I was not, of course, certain that the color was the same, just as I was not sure that I could assign the word 'dusky', in and of itself, a particular hue, but between the color of the squirrel's tail and the color of the hat which Father brought back from his years as a prisoner of war there could have stood an equal-sign. Father never spoke of the hat. We knew about every item of clothing in which he returned from the German camp – when he had been given the shirt, who gave him the pants, where he'd gotten the sweater—but the hat stubbornly remained outside all the stories. I even used to think at one time that it was a remnant of some brief but passionate love affair, one of the kind that many of the prisoners of war flew into while they waited, intoxicated by their new freedom, to go home. I could imagine the woman, drained by another death on another front, as she hands him the hat and says: "If you don't mean to stay, then would you at least take the hat?" Father hesitates. The oversized clothing that he received from the American soldiers hangs on him; the hat on his head, especially if it, too, is oversized, will certainly make him the butt of taunts. Nonetheless he reaches for it, the woman's finger and his touch for a moment on the brim, and then the hat changes owners. All this, of course, may have nothing to do with what happened. The hat may have turned up as part of one of the many trades that transpired among the internees themselves, but also later, among liberated prisoners, the local population and the allied soldiers, but what could Father have offered in exchange for the hat? And why this hat, of all things? Whatever the case, the hat showed an enviable durability. After Father's death, every time we sat down to discuss what to do with his things the hat would magically vanish from our lists. "Oh, leave it," we'd say and find a new perch for it in the wardrobe. Sometimes we'd take it out onto the courtyard balcony, shake it and brush it, and leave it to air. Mother always said it was a genuine miracle that, after all those years, moths had never gotten to it, while I kept complaining that it had no lining; had it a lining, I would have cut the lining open, ripped it out, and surely behind it I would have found Father's secret. I never doubted there was a secret, or rather I wanted there to be one, simply because a thing with no secret is more awful than a thing with a secret: concealing nothing, it actually conceals everything, and I didn't dare venture into such complexities in those first days after Father's death, while I ached for simple signposts. Time passed, the hat took its place on the highest shelf, popping up now and then in our conversations, usually when one of us, or one of our friends who knew about it, proposed a new theory for its history. Father's belongings vanished gradually from the bathroom, the closets, the coatrack, and the hat, along with photographs in the family album, became in time the focal presence of Father's absence. And then, one day, it was gone. No one, of course, knew how this happened. Mother, Sister and I, relatives and the friends who visited us often, all of us readily denied any implication in this, as my aunt called it, 'reprehensible affair', therefore making each of us a little, equally, suspect. Aside from this suspicion, I had to note the appealing symmetry in the secrecy surrounding Father's dusky hat: it was not known how it came, nor was it known how it left. The same can be said of my father, of each of us: from the unknown we come, to the unknown we go, and no one knows why we do, but sometimes objects tell us more than any living creature can. Sometimes the reverse is true, as it was just now when the squirrel stood up on its hind legs to take a new peanut. I looked at its dusky tail and thought that I would not be surprised if here, ten thousand kilometers from the place where it was last seen, I were to find Father's old hat. I even turned, as if it might be there behind me. It wasn't; nor was the squirrel when I turned back. What could I do? I picked up the scraps of peanut shell, stood up, and tossed them into the trash.

When you are getting to know a new man, take a look first at his nails. If, as the old saying goes, the eyes are the mirror of the soul, then the nails mirror the heart. I'm thinking of the fingernails, here, though toenails also matter. It is much harder, however, to find out anything about a person's toenails, you don't usually get a chance until retreat is no longer an option, when your clothes are in a heap by the bed. Even then, especially then, it is tricky to ask someone if you might have a look at his toes. I tried it once. The man looked me over —we were lying in bed in the dark and he came up pretty close, our noses touched—then he rolled over, flicked on the light, got dressed and left. I never saw him again. Later I found there were other ways, perhaps better left unsaid, suffice it to say that they often give me back and thigh aches. As soon as I realized that the toenails only substantiate what the fingernails tell me, I stopped. What is above is the same as what is below. I'm not sure whether that is another one of those old sayings, but it has never been proven wrong. In spite of everything, there are times when it is better to take me at my word.

My mother couldn't. "Whenever your father spoke," she said, "I believed him, and see me now."

I couldn't see anything. Actually, I could see a woman wondering where and how her life had gone by, but then everyone wonders that. Sooner or later a person wants to see where he's been and where he might yet go. It turns out he hasn't been anywhere and there is nowhere to go.

I couldn't say that to Mother, at least not while I watched how she sat in the kitchen, her hands in her lap, bent over photographs. She brought them out in a box which had held chocolate candies. There was a picture of two white kittens on the lid. One was sitting, while the other was reaching for a red rose with its paw. On the rose, as if glued in place, were three water droplets.

The photographs were sorted into several categories: "Pre-War," "Post-War," "The Occupation," "Weddings and Funerals," "Relatives." Each category was in a separate envelope. The first was the thickest;

the last held only three pictures: an uncle from Israel, an aunt from Canada, a picture of a gravestone from the Jewish cemetery in Šabac. The only picture which was not in one of the envelopes was of our dog, Ari, who was already old and refused to get up from the bedspread by the electric heater. In his eyes, Mother claimed, you could see death.

I couldn't tell her, at least not then, that you could see death in her eyes, too. Just as mirrors sometimes grow dark, tarnish, lose their depth, the soul grows stronger in the eyes, suspended, shadow-like, on the oily surface of death. The soul has actually taken the route that souls go, leaving the body behind to tramp around on earth, reeling and twitching like a chicken with its head cut off.

A mouse in your heart was one of my father's fancies. Whenever I started crying as a girl, he would crouch down beside me or take me in his arms or pull me into his lap, and say, "That mouse must be scampering around your heart again and making you cry." "Each touch of its paws," he'd say, "makes a tear. Go ahead and tell it: Scram, Mouse, and as soon as it is gone, the tears will stop."

And so they would. All I had to do was close my eyes, and say, "Scram, Mouse," and the patter of the little paws would fade somewhere beyond me, the way a door closes softly in the distance. Today, after so many years, whenever tears well up in my eyes, whether I'm sitting in a chapel or watching a soap opera on TV, I say those same words.

"That mouse must be pretty old by now," said my daughter when I tried to tell her the story. She came into the kitchen and found me sniffling over an open chocolate candy box and scattered photographs. "So old," she said, "it probably can barely drag its paws when it moves." Then she left.

I imagined how the mouse was perched on its hind legs at the bottom of my heart, peering up at me with its black eyes and twitching its whiskers inquisitively.

"Yes," I told him. "Your golden moment has come. You may stay."

My daughter came back. "Did you say something?" she asked.

I looked at her. Then I looked at a photograph on which my mother, very young, was leaning against a blossoming tree. Her face wore the same expression I had seen on my daughter's face Saturdays or Sundays, every time she came home late. When I came home late for the first time, Mother slapped me.

Anger, actually, wells from recognition. Ignorance spawns silence.

I didn't know that then, but I know it now. I still wasn't aware of it when my daughter was lurking somewhere behind my back while I flipped desperately through the scattered photographs, sure that somewhere in these slices of the past would be a trace that would help me.

I found nothing. In the distance, my daughter softly closed the door behind her. The same door the Mouse used to leave by, before.

ROBINS

TODAY DURING breakfast my nine-year-old son, as he did yesterday, slowly put his roll on the plate, closed his eyes, pressed his lips together, puffed his cheeks. And began to cry. He told me yesterday that he was crying because though March was nearly over, spring still hadn't come. He was afraid, he told me, that the ecological cycles he had been learning about at school would be disturbed, that there wouldn't be enough grass for the rabbits or enough rabbits for the coyotes. He was also afraid, he told me, that this spring, if it did ever come, he wouldn't be able to bury a sunflower seed in our back yard, water it and watch how it sprouts out of the ground and grows.

I try, just as I tried yesterday, to reassure him with stories of how seasons inevitably follow one after another in nature, about how everything has its time, as the ancient books say. I tell him that he will have to learn many things in life, but that patience is perhaps the most important of them all. "A person who can't wait," I say, "will hurt himself sooner or later, and then, with his impatience, hurt others, too."

The boy looks at me. From his tearful eyes I can see that he doesn't believe me.

I don't believe myself either (just as, when a boy, I didn't believe my own father). The winter is indeed so long that slowly but surely it turns into the 'winter of our discontent.' The snow that delighted us so last October, that thrilled us when it crunched underfoot, is blamed for everything, even the tiniest failure, especially all those faults we attribute to 'living abroad.' We'd be ready to give anything, actually, for sight of the first bunch of snowdrops. If they have snowdrops here. And if the snowdrops know how to push out from under all that snow.

Maybe because of that, says my wife, because of the relentless whiteness, all of our friends from 'home' continually talk about going back. When a person listens to them, he might think that back there where we come from it is never cold, snow never falls, and the roads are never iced over by freezing rain.

"Winter never lasts this long," says the boy, "I'm certain."

"And spring looks like spring," I add. "You needn't worry that if you blink you might miss it altogether."

My wife stops spreading butter on toast, looks first at me, then the boy, and says, "What is this? A male conspiracy?"

The boy doesn't answer. He is lost between his two languages and isn't certain of either any more. He wipes away the last tear with his forearm and brings the roll to his lips.

I keep quiet, but not because of language. I am quiet because of the images which pester me, the precision with which now, somewhere within me, I see every minute of my life because of an understanding I don't need any more, because of a decisiveness I can no longer muster.

"Nostalgia is a noun with a feminine ending," my wife says, "and don't you forget it."

"I don't know what you mean by that," says the boy, "but I do know exactly where all those toys of mine are that we left behind."

"And I know where my books are," I add.

My wife puts the bread and knife down on the plate. "And now I'm supposed to say," she says, "that I know where my rolling pin is, hmmm?"

"I bet it is still in the kitchen back in Zemun," answers the boy.

"If you say another word," my wife mutters through her teeth, "you will find out the hard way that I did bring one along with me."

"He who runs from the truth," I say, "comes back to the truth in the end."

"How would you know," she retorts, "are you some Chinese sage all of a sudden?"

"This is the realm of Indian shamans," I say. "Maybe I could turn into one of their totems."

"I'd like to be a turtle," says the boy.

"You see," says my wife, "it's because of those stories of yours that our child would rather be a reptile than a person."

"Turtles are amphibians," I reply, up in arms. "And what is so bad about turtles, anyway? People used to think that the whole world was borne on their backs. I even know a story about someone who was carried after a shipwreck for days by a giant sea turtle on its back until they reached land. And when we had some in our aquarium you fed them, changed their water, and cleaned their little castle."

"Only because none of you would," says my wife.

"Yes," pipes up the boy, "but when we went to Čortanovci on our excursion, and when we found that turtle down by the spring, you were the one who was holding it the whole time in your hands and whispering something in its ear."

"I did," says my wife, "but only because when you get the urge to whisper, you have to do it. Whose ear doesn't matter."

The boy and I exchange glances. I assume he has figured out, as I have, that the story about the ear and the whispering was actually meant for me, but since he has not, unlike me, been snagged yet by the web of subtextual meanings, he can freely return to eating his breakfast. I, on the other hand, am not able to recall a moment when her lips touched my earlobe, I push away the plate with the unfinished ham and cheese, and stand up.

"What's up," asks my wife, "appetite flagging all of a sudden?"

"Nope," I say while staring out the widow at the thick layers of snow and ice, but I'd give everything for one of those crescent rolls from that baker's at the marketplace.

"Or a piece of burek cheese pastry," says my wife, "do you remember how we used to go out at night for burek, and he'd curse as he handed it to us out the little window on the bakery door?"

The world turns back into a menu. Every time we confront our memories, it seems as if all of life consists of what sinks into our stomachs. We can no longer recall many faces, most places have faded like old postcards, but we remember vividly every pork chop stewed in sauerkraut, the roasts, the meat pastries, the walnut and poppy strudels.

Who knows how much longer we would have gone on kneading the dough of memories, when a couple of robins lit on the old willow in the yard. I showed them to my son. I reminded him how last spring and summer, every time after it rained, they plucked fat worms out of the damp earth. "They wouldn't have come," I tell him, "if they weren't certain to find those same tasty morsels again."

The boy is, momentarily, relieved. Then he grows solemn again. "But what," he asks, "if they are wrong?"

I reassure him and say that nature never errs. I promise that if the winter doesn't let up we will go out and buy worms and feed the robins, just as, during the winter months, we set out birdseed for the sparrows.

That appeases him. He pulls his hat down over his head, swings his book bag up onto his shoulder, and leaves for school. Through the window I see him halt under the willow and look up at the robins. His lips are moving, he is telling them something. I can imagine him comforting them now, feeling himself to be a master again of the events in the world around him.

The time will come when I will have to tell him that the 'winter of our discontent' may last far longer, and that the melting snow and ice needn't mean its end. Bitterness is a taste you have to sense, it doesn't matter whether the person is living in Alberta or Serbia. And that is why I would like to call to him that he should keep learning the mute language of animals and plants, that he needn't seek better friends. Unlike us, they do not know of good and evil and never do evil in the name of good. As far as they are concerned, winter is just one of the seasons. There can be no better teaching than that, son.

And as if he knows what is on my mind, he turns to me and waves.

SHADOWS

1.

WONDER OF WONDERS the train wasn't late; it pulled into the train station at P. precisely at four. There were no other travelers at the station, so for a moment Bogdan Marić thought it might be better not to get off the train at all, to stay on board instead and go on travelling to the last stop, to the provincial town of N., but nonetheless he dragged his suitcase along the corridor of the train car until he got to the door and lowered it down onto the platform. The suitcase was heavy with books, probably brought in vain, as he had done so many times before, but no point in crying over spilt milk, thought Bogdan as he straightened up and looked around. The train was already starting to pull out, the gears and chains were creaking, the wheels turning, the concrete under Bogdan's feet shuddered. Only when the train had vanished did Bogdan catch sight of the station hand: with his rolled-up red flag, tucked firmly under his arm, he was striding toward a door with the words "Station Manager" on it. He didn't so much as glance at Bogdan. The door slammed, the glass rattled, and a little later, in the corner of the window, the curtain moved. Somewhere there, thought Bogdan, is the station manager's eye. The curtain dropped, Bogdan leaned over, he grabbed the handle of the suitcase and moved slowly toward the exit that, if his memory served him well, led out into the square.

2.

The hotel was across the square, in the shade of several tall poplars. Bogdan had to stop three times as he crossed the square to catch his breath, rest his arm, and rub his blistered palm. If he were a poet perhaps this would be easier. It would definitely be easier, because one of his novels was like six or seven volumes of poetry, maybe more. And furthermore, poetry books are usually paperbacks, while his novels were hardbacks, sometimes even with a protective dust cover. He lifted his suitcase and strode the last twenty steps or so to the hotel. There he first saw the little poster announcing his reading: his name was spelled correctly, as were the titles of his books, but the photograph was blurred and gave the impression that Bogdan had a mustache and beard. Bogdan did not wear a beard, and he had only let his mustache grow out once, twenty years earlier, when he believed it might make him look older and more serious. He looked at the poster again, squinted, cocked his head to the side, but no matter what he did, the beard and mustache remained on the blurred face in the picture. "Free admission" it said on the bottom of the poster. Bogdan leaned his back on the glass door, pushed, and that was how he made his way into the vestibule of the hotel, backwards, dragging his suitcase after him, until he reached the reception desk. The reception desk was empty. Bogdan first coughed, then moved his suitcase with a scrape, and only then did he notice the bell. He lifted it up and banged it on the counter. Coming, said a woman's voice from behind the door, and then all went quiet again.

3.

When she appeared, the woman was younger than her voice had given him to think. In the corner of her lips, to the left, was a crumb of bread, and Bogdan could barely keep himself from brushing it off with his index finger. Instead, he gave her his name and said that he had been informed there would be a room reserved for him. The woman said she would take a look; she pulled a large register from under the counter and began leafing through it. The crumb slid from her cheek, tumbled over the opened pages and dropped to the floor. Bogdan couldn't see it as it fell, but he could imagine it dropping into emptiness, into a netherworld ruled by human feet. Yes, said the woman, the room is waiting for you. She turned and took a key down from a board on the wall. Number 14, she said, first floor. Only later, when Bogdan had already shoved his suitcase into the elevator, did she give him an envelope someone had left for him, on which his name was printed in block letters.

4.

Room no. 14 was in a shambles as were most of the hotel rooms in the Serbian interior. The lamp by the bed didn't work; the sockets had been yanked from the walls and bare electric wires poked from the jagged holes; spiderwebs hung from the high corners; the walls were scratched and scribbled, and stained dark with tobacco smoke; water dripped in the bathroom; the plastic lid on the toilet bowl had cracked all the way across and was tied by string to the plumbing pipes. Twenty-three years ago, when he had last stayed in P., the rooms at this hotel—perhaps it was this very room!—seemed almost luxurious havens compared to the provincial humdrum of life going on at the time. In the meanwhile, however, the war had happened, everything had changed, as if someone had spun the table, and now in front of those who were still sitting in the same seats as before were glasses or plates that were not, in fact, theirs. And so it was that the town of P., which had once nestled comfortably in the heart of the country, was now not far from the border, on a road that inevitably ended in N., where, Bogdan sensed, things were even worse, and where the hotel, if it was still standing, had been turned into a shelter for refugees. He sat in the faded armchair and opened the envelope he had received from the girl at the reception desk. He took out the sheet of paper, opened it and read the sentence, also printed in block letters: Call me, please. Underneath, instead of a signature, was a telephone number.

5.

Bogdan had been expecting a woman's voice, so when a man answered the phone his first urge was to hang up. Then he said his name and said he had just arrived. I know, said the man, I saw you.

Bogdan thought of the eye of the station manager, the curtain that
moved, the doorway full of dark shadows. I wanted to ask, the man
continued, if you might set aside some time for me after the reading.
Bogdan said nothing. I would like to show you something, said the
man, this won't take long, ten minutes, maybe less. Bogdan couldn't
settle on how old the man was, but sensed, particularly because of
the pleading that was coloring his voice, that it must be about a hefty
manuscript, which he would be asked to read and furnish with a
glowing review. Don't worry, said the man, as if he had been reading
Bogdan's thoughts, I won't ask you for recommendations for publica-
tion. They told me that after my reading there would be a dinner,
Bogdan replied, and that was his last defense. Ten minutes, said the
man, perhaps not even that. Ten minutes, Bogdan repeated and hung
up, peeved with himself for agreeing even to that much.

6.

He went down to the foyer of the hotel, left his key on the counter of
the reception desk, and went out. The beard and mustache were still
prominent on his blurred photograph, perhaps even a little longer
and thicker than they had been when he arrived. There was no one
out in the square. A dog appeared from behind a distant tree, went
over to another tree, raised its leg and left its mark, then vanished.
Bogdan walked slowly across the square, closer to the train station,
where he had always found good coffee on a side street, at least as
long as he could remember, in the garden of a small restaurant. He
did not turn to look around as he walked, but out of the corner of his
eye he kept track of the windows, curtains and shelters of shadows.
Nothing moved, though the observer might be exceptionally skil-
ful, because the smaller the town, thought Bogdan, the greater the
skill, reaching true art, at peering through holes and cracks. When he
turned onto the side street, he saw that he had been wrong: there was
no trace of a restaurant, only a glassed-in entrance to an agricultural
pharmacy. He went over to the street across the way, and peered into
another two, but reality was implacable and completely different from

his recollections. He returned to the hotel. By the porter's stand, leaning on the counter, the director of the library was waiting for him.

7.

Bogdan felt better at the library, surrounded by dusty books. He sipped at a strong, aromatic homemade brandy that an old librarian poured for him in a largish glass, all trembling that she was welcoming an eminent writer. Meanwhile the director of the library spoke of the history of the library, the publishing activities that had dwindled during the war years, the members who could no longer afford their library dues, the annual anthology put out by local poets who still published it every May 1st despite adversity, and a puppet theater festival that had moved to P. from M. after the new borders were established, thanks to one of the members of the festival selection committee who was now a refugee. Bogdan nodded, he felt the warmth of the brandy filling the cavity beneath his knee. Then someone came into the library director's office, first a woman in a trench coat, then a man in a green blazer, and finally a young woman came in from the local radio station who took Bogdan into the stacks, where they would be able, in peace and quiet, she said, to talk about the fate of the artist in these troubled times. Bogdan spent some ten minutes hunched over her tape recorder, staring at her nails, done in black nail polish. Have you ever written poetry? the young woman asked. Now that is something, Bogdan answered, that we could discuss after the reading. He didn't look up, but he covered the microphone opening on her cassette player with the tips of his fingers.

8.

In the poorly lit reading room, the faces of the audience were shadowy. The girl from the local radio station sat in the first row; all the others—twelve of them, Bogdan counted—took seats in the back rows, by the door. He tried to spot the man who had sent him the message, but soon he had to give up, they were all equally suspicious, probably because of the plentiful shadows. The director of the library said a few sentences about Bogdan's books, he mentioned the major prizes, announced that the collected works would be out soon, and mentioned that this reading was planned as a conversation between the author and his readers, so that after Bogdan had read a passage from his most recent novel, they would be free to ask questions. And buy my books, Bogdan added, laughing. No one responded with laughter except the elderly librarian, in charge of selling the books that were laid out on a table, who leaned over them, as if grieving in advance for each book that would be purchased. Bogdan read his favorite passage: after the battle, warriors are resting, some treating their wounds, some writing letters, the war is, in fact, over and the world is new and pure, justice has prevailed, life goes on, no, Bogdan corrected himself, or rather his hero did, life had never been interrupted, life is stronger than death, even those who died, who gave their lives for our better today, for a different tomorrow, they are not actually dead, they live in all of us, they never stop humming in our blood and our memories, and if love happens to us, if we feel passion again lift our tired thighs, everything will be good, no, everything will be better, better than it ever was before. And now, said the library director, let's have some questions. Silence settled on the reading room. The director coughed two or three times; clearly he was uncomfortable, but Bogdan, to tell the truth, didn't care. After the reading, interpretations were always unimportant. And precisely when he was about to whisper to the director to wrap up the reading, one hand went up into the air. Yes, said the director. A young blond man, in a raincoat, began to speak even before he had stood up. He would like to know, he said, what the eminent guest thought of a text that had appeared in the periodical *Truth* in which there was extensive coverage of an alleged intimate and tragic affair the writer had had with a certain person from our town. Bogdan made no effort to conceal his rage: A lot of nonsense, he said, with only one purpose—to undermine the struggle for a genuine, true patriotism, and to show us, completely dedicated to these efforts, in the worst possible light. Meaning, the

young man went on, that there was no secret connection, no trag-
edy? A disturbed woman took her life, that is all, said Bogdan. The
director of the library applauded, and everyone else followed suit,
but the applause was brief and ended while Bogdan was still wondering whether or not he should bow as a sign of his gratitude.

9.

Only when the young blond man addressed him again at the reading
room exit did Bogdan recognize the voice he had conversed with that
afternoon on the phone. The young man was not, indeed, carrying
any sort of manuscript; Bogdan could breathe a sigh of relief. The
young man said that it would be best for them to go to Bogdan's
room. He wouldn't be taking much of his time, he said, just a couple
of minutes. Bogdan was hungry and sleepy and he wanted to sit down
to eat as soon as possible, but the young man dismissed his suggestion
that they find a table in some corner of the café where Bogdan would
be taken to dinner. Five, maybe ten minutes at the outside, said the
young man, but alone, please. Bogdan agreed finally, and he and the
young man went across the square to the hotel. There was no one
at the reception desk, so Bogdan had to take his key from the board
himself. They went up the stairs and into the room. The young man
sat in the armchair; Bogdan settled down on the bed. There, thought
Bogdan, while other writers are bringing girls to their rooms, I am
here entertaining a young man who doesn't know what he is doing.
The young man looked up, and straight into Bogdan's eyes. That
woman, he said, so she was crazy. Bogdan didn't know what the
young man was talking about for a moment; then he remembered.
Crazy as they come, she didn't know what she was doing. The young
man said nothing. Bogdan felt a stab of pain in his gut. If he didn't
eat something soon, he knew, he wouldn't be able to sleep tonight.
The young man raised his eyes to Bogdan: She was my mother, he
said. Bogdan swallowed. And she wasn't crazy, the young man went
on, she just wanted someone to really love her. Bogdan wanted to
say: I loved her, but there was no time left for lies. The young man

shoved his hand into his pocket: This is what I wanted to show you, he said. Bogdan looked down at the young man's hand and saw a grenade. He had read about grenades like this: the soldiers had been bringing them back from the war and selling them cheap. The young man squeezed it with his other hand and pulled out the pin. Bogdan thought that he ought to get up, then he could just see himself buzzing around like a headless fly, along the walls, across the floor, under the bed, along the ceiling, as he lunged at the window and rebounded off the door, as he called for help through the little window of the peephole, and then instead he settled deeper into the bed, leaned back on the pillow and looked up. If I watch closely, he thought, I'll see the hanging lamp sway.

ALL EMIGRÉ stories boil down to a couple of sentences, to the two words: departed, arrived, as my acquaintance Branko Grujić often said. He'd get so animated whenever he spoke of this, he would look silly, tall and skinny, so flushed as he repeated the words over and over, gesticulating with his arms like a windmill. Departed, arrived, Branko Grujić would sing, that is all there is to say, it made no difference to him that the starting and end points were different, that it took some people two days of travel while others journeyed for weeks, even years. His arms would stop mid-air from time to time, as if the wind had suddenly died down, and he'd ask me, Where is it you're from? And then I'd tell him as I had so many times before about my journey, which I was sick of relating, I'd been through it a hundred times at least, and not just for him, but for everyone who wanted to hear, and now I was tired of it, nothing happened in that story, it was ruler-straight like the Saskatchewan highway, and, worst of all, it ended up nowhere. It hung there in a void, just as I was suspended in a void, and I looked to myself like a leg of meat that had been hung out for curing, and which, despite the sun and rain and snow, would not dry. I didn't tell Branko Grujić everything, but, with a little mystery, would reply, From there to here. I left there; came here. So anyone who doesn't know where the 'there' and the 'here' are has nothing to look for in this story, and most certainly has never met Branko Grujić, who kept swinging his arms like a windmill, though there was no wind, not a cloud in the sky, no rustling of leaves in the trees, no apples dropping into tall grass, no Canadian geese honking, there weren't any spiders inching down a thread, there wasn't even gravel crunching on the shore. But Branko Grujić repeated, So where is it that you're from, was it Odžaci? I pretended to be clueless about the location of the town of Odžaci, though I've been there a thousand times, it was always on my way to somewhere, but the fact of the matter was that I am not from Odžaci, nor am I from Dimnjak, if such a place exists, nor am I from Peć, and furthermore I explained that since both Odžaci and Dimnjak mean chimney, and Peć means oven, and I am not from any of them, I am not a fellow of fire, smoke, kindling, charcoal and tree stumps. I said to him that I am from a cold place—which is not, of course, true, but then again you can claim that for anything—I mean that it isn't true, from which might follow that lying is fine, because, after all, there is no truth. What do you mean, asked Branko Grujić, and his arms swung faster because he was bothered; he had learned that you are always supposed to tell the truth, that the Lord isn't up in heaven for nothing, that he is there to peek down and check to see who is lying and who isn't and then for those who lie he arranges for life in the netherworld among the black devils and for the lover of truth he keeps a place at his feet in heaven. Now you decide, said Branko Grujić, where you would rather end up. Well, my man, I say to him, I have been to hell several times and I've always come back; it is my turn to go to heaven now, so I can see what it's like, if the fruit trees are as big as some say they are, though I hesitate to believe them, and if the women are really naked, I mean they have that leaf down below but their breasts are bare, so sometimes paradise looks like one great, big, wobbly breast, all undulating like the sea. But you've never seen the sea in your life, have you, I asked Branko Grujić, so you can't even begin to imagine a breast that big, with a nipple the size of an elephant's trunk, and he shouted, But I can, I can, who says I can't, and he swung his arms around faster and faster, so fast, in fact, that I got a little scared that his arms might snap right off and fly away, each on its own, heavenward. They weren't wrong when they told me not to exaggerate, not only about the breasts, but about all other animals, traits and descriptions. Language has to be simple when it comes to Branko Grujić, and if someone starts confusing him with language, making mountains out of molehills, that person is risking, they told me, a short circuit of the brain, not the brain of the person taking the risk, but of Branko Grujić's brain, in which even simple sentences tangle, and it is much worse with compound and complex sentences, not to speak of complicated exclamatory sentences. If you are feeling great, for example, don't shout: Damn it, I feel great, because that confuses Branko Grujić, and he asks: How could you be feeling great if you just shouted 'Damn it'? Good question, absolutely, though it isn't our fault, it is language that turns itself inside out like a glove, and everything that is in it becomes the opposite, only I won't get into examples here, there are plenty, more than I need, but let someone else write about that, I have enough on my hands with this problem I have with Branko Grujić and those arms of his. Branko, I once asked him, are you an airplane? He froze, stared at me with those big eyes of his, and then put his index finger to his temple as if to ask: What is up with you? Are you crazy? Later he leaned over confidentially to say that the wings on airplanes didn't flap, every baby knew that, so he was no plane, he was a flying platform. It hadn't been invented yet, he added, and he was the one and only prototype, and if it worked out well, then probably everyone will be made into a platform, it would just take time. And here he showed me with his fingers, with his thumb and fingers he grasped a chunk of air and raised it so that I could see it, and indeed, he was talking about a little time, it would pass quickly, quicker than we thought. Well, I said then, I am not sure I would like to be a platform, let alone a flying one, but he shook his head and said that no one would ask. I would just get up one morning and start swinging my arms, that is how it had happened to him, no one asked him, he simply opened his eyes, got up, stood in front of the mirror and began swinging his arms. And then he knew, he said. What did he know, I asked, could he remember? And he stopped to think, put his hand to his forehead and rolled his eyes, but there was nothing that came to mind, he said, just a question. Let's hear it, I said. He looked at me, squinted, his eyes got all small, and he asked me whether I was from Odžaci. I am not, I said to him, I have told you that a hundred times, I am from a place where fire doesn't burn, where ice singes the fingers like a flame, and I took the scholastic atlas and showed him the far north, way up above Saskatchewan, and he looked, shook his head, said he could never live there, especially if it were far from Odžaci, and I told him it was, that he would have to fly twelve hours to get there, and he started trotting around as if getting the momentum to take off, as if he were preparing to roll down a runway, and then he stopped and said, Boy am I crazy, a platform doesn't need momentum, a platform flies straight up in the sky, and he started stretching until he was standing on his tiptoes, and that is how he stood, in perfect balance, and whoever wanted to could see that he, Branko Grujić, the person-platform, was flying through the air as no one had ever flown before him, even Nikola Tesla, whom they say did more than everyone else combined, and even if he couldn't fly as much, he could a little, that is what Mihajlo Pupin had seen, but he didn't dare write it down in his autobiography so that others wouldn't think he was crazy, and he might have thought the same thing had he read the autobiography later, and come to that part. By the time he'd be able to remember, his reason would have fled him forever, better let sleeping dogs lie, better not taunt destiny, better not pour oil on the fire, there are things to learn and things to forget, things to shove deep down inside so that it looks as if they aren't inside you any more, that they are gone. Pupin knew that, I say to Branko Grujić, but Tesla didn't. Whatever occurred to him, he said, it didn't matter who stumbled across it, Tesla gave everything away, in hatfuls and handfuls. There weren't enough hats, he was said to have claimed, to hold everything he could come up with. I don't know if that is the truth, I said to Branko Grujić, but he slowed down the swinging of his arms, you could plainly see that he had slowed down and was freezing up, and he whispered to me confidentially that Tesla was the first man-platform, that there was footage about it in some American intelligence service, the difference being that Tesla didn't flap his arms, but rather moved around using his mind. It is a well known fact, said Branko Grujić and sped up a little, that Tesla read the newspaper on the kitchen table from the dining room, though there were three walls, a wardrobe and a cupboard between him and the newspaper. Then Branko Grujić got serious and I knew what was coming next, he would ask me if I was from Odžaci, so I said to him, Listen, don't ask me, I am not from Odžaci, I have never been there, I never intend to go there, there are plenty of people in Odžaci without me. Branko Grujić said nothing, and blinked. And you, I asked him, would you like to go to Odžaci? There is nothing I would like more, he said, and began slowing down again, he'd spent his whole life there, all thirty-seven years, and he could not imagine spending another thirty-seven years in Saskatchewan. Fuck Saskatchewan, what is there here they don't have in Odžaci, say one thing, though I needn't make the effort, because he knew there wasn't anything, just as he knew there were things that your heart desires that can't be found in Saskatchewan or in Regina, first of all plums. I shrugged, I don't know anything about plums in Saskatchewan, but there must be some, everywhere there are plums, however Branko Grujić stuck to his guns, he took me to the window, he pointed to the trees in the front yard, and the trees on the other side of the street, and if I were to see a single plum tree, he said, report it to him. I have never reported anyone, I told him, and I'm not going to start reporting plums. Branko Grujić stopped, his arms dropped to his side, his chin dropped to his chest, his knees buckled a little, as if he had gotten heavier all of a sudden or more vulnerable to the force of gravity, or had he simply run out of steam, the platform had to run on some kind of fuel, didn't it? I would like to think about this but I haven't the time, because I hear a voice calling us, first Branko, then me, and when we turn around we see that woman from the Immigration and Refugee Board who gets paid to talk to us in our language, and then translates everything she hears into their language and that helps them decide what to do with us, not together, but one by one, because that is how we arrived, first he got here from Odžaci, then I came from that other place, and we ran into each other in a Saskatchewan city park right next to a children's playground where he was swinging his arms around wildly and reciting "The Three Rovers." He was reciting so nicely, with such feeling, that I felt as if I were out there in that dark and stormy night, and I imagined that I would never leave him again, that I would always be with him, but if that woman continued to pester us, and if the Secreteriat for Emigrants and Refugees continued to give us a hard time, then I would head out with him into the prairie, into the thicker and thicker grass, and we would walk and walk until we vanished over the horizon. I would rather go to Odžaci, said Branko Grujić when I put my idea to him, and then I answered him that that was fine, we could go to Odžaci, but first we'd head north to where I had showed him in the school atlas and then later we could go to Odžaci if he still wanted to, because once you go north, they say, you stay there forever. I described all this to the woman, and not just once, more than once, the very first time she came, and then I figured out that there was no point to my words, I was even speaking slowly so that I could be sure that she heard me, I even repeated some of the more difficult words several times, like abyss, criminal, *gibanica* and dandelion. She didn't know how to say *gibanica* in English, so then I told her that if there were a word for *gibanica* in English, then it would no longer be English, so it was better not to sweat the translation, and she definitely shouldn't translate *gibanica* as "cheese pastry". She shot me an angry glance and said cheese is cheese, to which I replied angrily that cheese is not cheese, just as Saskatchewan is not the same as Odžaci, and that we'd best give up on the whole idea, because otherwise who knows what might happen. And then I told her how Branko Grujić and I would go out into the prairie, maybe even beyond, way up north, and the very next day they separated us, put us in different rooms, at the opposite ends of the building, and it took another few weeks before they let us spend time again together, and all that time the woman was coming and looking at us from the door and smiling as if she had figured it all out. She hasn't figured out squat, Branko Grujić said, she can go right ahead standing by that door for days but she will never understand anything. His arms abruptly ceased swinging and he stopped like a windmill dreaming wind. His hair bristled, his lips twisted, his tongue stuck out, first his eyes filled with tears and then they bugged out like never before, and I thought that the moment had come to kiss him on his cold forehead, but when I came closer and brushed his skin with my lips, I jerked back as if I'd been singed, his forehead was so hot. Then he rushed at that woman and the closer he got to her, the more wildly his arms flailed, but I wasn't watching any more, something drew my attention in the yard, a cat or maybe a mouse, or maybe a leaf shook on a branch, and when it stopped interesting me, I looked over their way but there was no one there any more, the woman or Branko Grujić, and after I began asking the staff, it turned out that no one had seen them, as if they had disappeared without a trace, which is impossible, there is no one who can out and out disappear, least of all a person-platform, that miracle of science, a man of the future, though Branko Grujić was more a man of the past, because he never could shake off what had happened, not even when he was no longer certain where he was from. I remember when he came over to me that first time, his lips pursed as if he were getting ready to whistle, and he asked me if I was from Odžaci. He cut me to the quick, but I managed to stay cool and, without a blink, say I was not from Odžaci, that I had never even been there. He looked at me with unmasked suspicion and said he was sure he knew me from Odžaci. He scowled, and you could almost hear him thinking. Then he stopped thinking, his arms started to swing, and I could breathe a sigh of relief. The woman appeared only later that evening, shaking and in tears. She couldn't speak, she was sobbing so hard. And while the patients and staff were gathering around her, she pointed upward into the air above her and cursed god in all the languages she knew. Then some of us started to applaud, then the others joined in, so I did, too, though reluctantly, because I didn't know where Branko Grujić was, and none of the words I thought were able to tell me.

I WOKE UP on Friday with a pain in my left shoulder. It was a dull throb, only slightly worse than the discomfort caused, I thought, by sleeping funny, for which I ultimately blamed the mattress. Old, tattered and misshapen, it should have been traded in long ago. The stab of shoulder pain, deep, nearly buried, was, I sensed, my last warning.

During the day as I hurried through various duties the pain waned or I paid it no mind, but in the early evening when I was on my way home there it was again. I took off my suit jacket and when I swung back my left arm the pain in my shoulder, flashing and suddenly sharp, stopped my movement halfway. I stood there in front of the mirror, legs akimbo and leaning slightly forward, and I could see myself frowning as I sucked air through my teeth and grimacing lips. Then I lowered my arms and the jacket slid off them straight to the floor.

I went to the bathroom and took two tablets for the pain. I warmed up a slice of lasagna and ate it sitting in the armchair in front of the television set while watching the news and the sports chronicle. I drank an apple juice. When I got up and went into the kitchen to leave my plate the pain was gone. Without letting go of the fork, I carefully raised my left arm high above my head, then gingerly bent it behind my back making sure not to let the tines of the fork touch my shirt. The anchorman was reading the sports scores and did not look up from the sheet of paper that was shaking ever so slightly in his hands. When he did look up at the camera the pain came shooting back full force like a clap of thunder after a deceptive silence, heralded by a lightning flash. I stumbled, my plate dropped from my grasp, bits of pasta and ground meat flew all over the throw rug. The pain subsided right away, muted, and when I leaned over to pick up the crumbs I felt it only as a shimmering reflection of actual pain, a presentiment of hardship lost in the labyrinth of the shoulder joint.

Some people can tolerate pain but I am not one of them. When something hurts, I wait briefly, take a tablet or two, hold a heated or chilled cloth on the ache, and if the pain doesn't go away I head straight for the doctor. So that is what I did this time. I did not want to stumble again, fearing another jolt, so off I hurried instead to the walk-in clinic in the neighboring block, right next to a sporting goods store.

There were four people in the waiting room: a mother with a little girl, a young man, his hand wrapped in a bloody bandage, an elderly woman who was dozing. The little girl, as far as I could tell, had an earache in her left ear, her head was bent to the side and she was pressing a terrycloth towel to her ear. Her mother whispered in her other ear: telling her a story, maybe to chase away gloomy thoughts or simply keep the child from falling asleep. The little girl was nodding, and only then did I see the occasional tear welling in the corners of her eyes.

The receptionist at the reception desk had ruddy cheeks. She asked me what my name was, why I was there and had I ever been to the clinic before. I answered. She asked me, also, how long my shoulder had been hurting and whether this had ever happened before. I told her that the pain began that morning, that it woke me from sleep before the alarm clock went off on my bedside table, and that this had never happened before. And the other shoulder, asked the receptionist, what about that one? We both looked at my right shoulder, but before I had a chance to say anything, a doctor appeared at the door to the office and called someone's name. That's me, said the woman with the little girl. She got up and steered the girl into the office. In the silence the old woman's quiet snoring was suddenly audible. "We have three doctors on duty this evening," said the receptionist, "you won't be waiting long."

And sure enough, I had only taken my seat when another door opened. The young man with the bloody bandage got up and walked over to it even before the blond doctor called his name. The old woman moved and smacked her lips. Her right hand slid from her lap and swung above a crumpled tissue on the floor. Under the chair where the young man with the bloody bandage had been sitting there were several small irregular dark spots. A poster on the wall warned of the danger of smoking. Another poster listing the symptoms of depression hung by the window. A coat rack languished in the corner. A low table was scattered with magazines and newspapers. There was a partway-finished crossword puzzle over which a plastic cup, full of water, cast a long shadow.

The door of the third office creaked and a wan girl appeared in the doorway. She went over to the receptionist at the front desk and said something to her in a soft voice. The receptionist smiled. She touched the girl's arm. The girl turned and walked toward the exit. When she reached the glass door she leaned on it and pushed it with her whole body. For an instant the waiting room was filled with the sounds of the nighttime traffic and then the receptionist called my name. I looked first at her then at the slumbering old woman, but the receptionist shook her head. She said that the old woman slept there a few hours every night and then she'd leave, no need to worry that I was taking her place in line.

I stood and went into the office. The doctor, a large young woman, was sitting at a small desk. She looked at the sheet of paper on the desk before her and then asked me the same questions I had answered for the receptionist. I gave her my name and that I was here because of a pain in my left shoulder, that I always came to this clinic when I had an emergency. "How long has it been hurting?" asked the doctor. I told her the shoulder started hurting that morning, early, before my alarm clock went off, and then when I woke up I couldn't get back to sleep. "Has that happened before?" the doctor wanted to know. "Never," I said, "this is a first." The doctor turned over the sheet of paper but there was nothing on the other side. "And the other shoulder," she asked, "what about that one?" We both looked at my right shoulder as if it might tell us something. "That one is fine," I said. "I hope," I added. The doctor noted something on the bottom of the piece of paper and said, "All of us need a little hope." Then she got up.

She wasn't just large, she was tall. If she had come over to me then, my head would have probably reached only to her chin, but first she told me to sit on the examination table that was draped in a white sheet. The table was also high, and to get up onto it I first had to step on a metal footstool attached to the foot of the table. So then our faces, when she did come over to me, were at the same height.

She told me to extend both arms straight out in front, and then she studied them, turning her head first to the left, then to the right. Then she asked me to raise my arms up toward the ceiling, to move them back behind me, to swing them like propellers. After each of these movements she asked me to describe any discomfort I might feel, if I did feel any, and the way in which the pain was different from the pain I'd felt, if I had feel it, in the previous position. Then she told me again to stretch them out in front of me, first with the palms facing down and then facing up. She dropped a pencil onto my palms and it jiggled gently, as if tugged by an invisible thread. The doctor took the pencil and tucked it behind her ear. She touched my fingertips and asked if I had noticed a change in how sensitive they were. "No," I said, though actually I wasn't sure. The doctor described an invisible line on my left palm with the tip of the fingernail on her right index finger. "Do you feel that?" she asked. I nodded. Then she drew a line on my left palm. "And that?" "Maybe a little less," I said. "Maybe is not an answer," said the doctor. She squeezed my right thumb, then the left. "Any difference here?" she asked. I didn't know. The doctor sighed and shook her head. Then she stepped closer, reached over and took me by the wrists and pulled my hands to her breasts. "Now," she said, "any difference now?" I tried to focus on my hands, first on the right one, then on the left, but all I wanted was to close my eyes, nothing else. The doctor lifted my thumbs and lowered them onto the tips of her breasts. "Left thumb, right thumb," she said, "how is that?" I gently squeezed her left nipple with my right thumb, then with my left thumb I squeezed her right nipple. There was something confusing in the switching of sides, connecting the opposite poles of the bodies, but I had to admit that under each thumb I could feel her nipples harden slowly and lurch against the fabric of her blouse. "No difference?" asked the doctor. "None," I said. "Sure?" "I'm sure," I said. I could stay like this, I thought, to the end of my days with my hands resting on her breasts, but then she moved and stepped back, sat down at the desk and began to write. My arms stayed in the same position for a time as if suspended by invisible threads and then they fell, dropped into my lap.

Just then someone knocked at the door. The doctor opened it and the voice of the receptionist could be heard telling her that they had brought in a child who had a nosebleed that couldn't be staunched. The doctor looked at me, said I should wait and closed the door after her. My first thought was to go over to the desk and see what she had written, but I was afraid I wouldn't be able to climb back up onto the examination table if she were to come back too soon. I swung my legs a little, peered into the corners of the office and at the traces of dust on the grimy glass of the glaring neon tubes. On the wall to the right of the door there was a large clock. A red jacket hung on the coat rack. In a wastepaper basket by the desk there were discarded plastic gloves and crumpled pieces of paper. Over the sink was a mirror. On the ceiling I noticed two sprinkler heads in case of fire. The floor was clean. I swung my legs again. I had nothing more to look at and I thought it would be best for me to close my eyes. I closed them. Somewhere from deep in my belly, perhaps deeper yet, I began to be swept by a great weariness. It wiggled along my spine, sneaked inbetween my legs and under my armpits, pressed my neck, rumbled in my ears. I slowly lowered myself onto the examination table, on my right side, propping my head with my right hand. I raised my legs but didn't straighten them. Curled up, I'll fall asleep more easily, I thought. Then there were footsteps, but I didn't open my eyes. I knew she was bringing me a blanket. They surely wouldn't let me get cold here.

MY NAME IS Adam and I do not know why I'm here. Here: in a city standing indecisively between the Rocky Mountains and the Great Prairie, not at one with snowy peaks or the grassy plain, always at the cusp of the divide, on the cutting edge of difference.

In a sense all this began as a joke, or at least I now see it was a joke I was playing on myself, though then, when it began, it was tinged with a grave sense of resolve. When we distance ourselves enough from watershed moments each of us demonstrates an awe-inspiring capacity for altering the past and falsifying history. I remember how miserable this made me feel a few years back while I was still in my former country, when our propaganda machine began to chug full steam, manufacturing an array of chronicles of honor and dishonor. Then it hit me that I was doing the same thing, even if more innocent matters were in question: a present with no objective vantage point—for there is no such vantage point—can hardly produce an objective past; instead the past is composed of the same number of small, smooth surfaces, a little darkened, perhaps, like an old mirror, that make up the multiple face of the present.

Of course I did not come up with this right away. Days, weeks, months went by, there were cities reduced to rubble, people became numbers on lists, cows wandered around the devastated lands and gazed at the pale moon. Life turned into a department store where any number of versions of the past were on display. Some were attractively packaged, others were crude and coarse, but everyone was supposed to buy one. A person, like me, who opted for passing through the store and going out the other side with no purchase in hand ended up, slowly but surely, alone. Men recoiled, women showed no kindness, children looked straight through him as if he were not there.

And indeed he was not there: I was not there. And that is why perhaps from this point everything starts seeming like a joke. Here, where every sense of self merges with the over-ample space, this convulsive attachment to something which, as they say on serious television shows, "defines identity," had to look pretty silly. In vain friends and acquaintances knocked on my door, called me on the phone, ran into me in the street.

"Life exists," they said, "only when you see it in its historical continuity, the present is not a magic carpet winging you through time and space, the only person who will have a future is the person who in it sees the re-shaping of the past."

I kept quiet and retreated into my loneliness. Mine was no noble solitude that a person chooses of his own volition, but rather an accursed apartness imposed by others. In short, no matter where I turned I was met by a void: people stepped aside as I walked by and sidestepped my destination. The only things left for me were the dead ones.

And so it was that one day I got onto a city bus, went to the Canadian Embassy, and took my place in line. I filled out the first form, returned home, waited, received new forms, filled them out, waited again, went for a doctor's examination, picked up all the necessary documents, was interviewed, shook hands, signed for receipt of an emigrant visa, bought an airline ticket. All those verbs, the string of independent clauses, all of that was accompanied at the time by gravity and determination, even a feeling of the inevitability of destiny. Only later, here, did I begin to see that the whole time I was believing it was actually a kind of joke, that I was waiting in lines, going for interviews and holding my breath for the X-ray only so I could mock someone, that I could show that, aside from the present, nothing else existed, least of all the past, especially a past we choose ourselves.

Now I wonder: what did I choose? I cannot give the right answer. Everything I come to, regardless of whether I am standing in front of a window or walking along endless streets or staring into a mirror, is: silence.

At first, in this city, while I hurried from office to office, filled out forms and was assigned an array of numbers instead of my name (and my former life, of course) in powerful computer systems, I had the feeling that something was opening. I didn't know what. The images I thought in were simple, like: life is a corridor lined with doors, or: life is a stage, or: eyes are the mirror of the soul, the heart is a machine, the stomach is a sack, a dream is a post-card from a journey, I am someone else.

Then I felt I was falling: I sank, and over me, with a slam, lids and shutters clanged shut. When the first snow fell, the whiteness blinded me. When ice covered the river I went out on a bridge, took off my cap and gloves, and let the frost bite me. The sun neared the far-off mountains and day became night.

This didn't worry me, I thought. In a certain sense it is easier to walk in darkness than in light. You needn't worry about anything. You can be naked, who you really are.

All of this was, of course, pure denial, futile stabs at finding comfort, and I talk about it all now when words have long since lost their meaning and when every word, when said aloud, sounds foreign and I have to look it up in dictionaries.

In fact, the determination drained from me while I was still on board the plane. As I flew I thought I was getting further and further from a seething chasm that was caving in on itself, but, unawares, I was getting closer and closer to another chasm, one hidden inside me, every bit as seething and hollow, every bit as subject to doubts and uncertainties. When I stepped off the plane, straight into a freezing north wind, I swayed in my clothing like a straw scarecrow. Only my heavy shoes, kept me on the ground; with their weight, everything else was gone.

I rented an apartment in the northern part of town, on the margins of the artistic quarter. The apartment was small: a bedroom, living room, kitchen and bathroom. The walls were bare, the floors covered in worn carpeting, the windows curtainless. Next to the refrigerator hung an outdated promotional calendar. Beyond the sliding glass doors, on the terrace, two plastic chairs were collecting dust.

There is always an easy way to see whether a place can truly become a home, as my mother used to say. You buy a plant in a flower pot and try keeping it alive. If you succeed, get a cat. If you do not, there is no furniture or hearth that will warm your soul. But watch out, she said, each person has his own plant, each person must cultivate his own flower.

So, OK, I thought, my plant, my flower. I found a florist shop and in I went. From the dozens of potted flowers, flower arrangements, bouquets and wreaths of dried flowers spread a close, oily smell. Cactuses, exotic blossoms, vines, violets, rubber plants, nettles—never before in such bounty, I was fearful that I would not find myself. Then my eyes lit on a cyclamen. I knew nothing of cyclamens, or rather I knew nothing about any of the flowers, and the salesperson, when I asked her, only smiled and shrugged. All you need to know is on the tag, she said. The tag said: Keep out of direct sunlight; do not water excessively; do not keep in the dark.

I could not imagine why anyone would want to keep a cyclamen, or any other plant for that matter, in the dark, but these three commandments became the foundation of my being. Everything was subjected to them: my first activity in the morning, my last gaze in the evening, my movements during the day, my search for work, hamburgers and pizza in stand-up joints, in malls, beer when I came home, staring at the muted television set which had I turned around, just in case, so that I might reduce the influence of its ghostly radiation. I bought a watering can, a small bottle with mineral nutrient additives, a miniature set of gardening tools—a little spade, hoe, and rake—for working the soil: the only thing I couldn't find was a handbook on cultivating cyclamen plants. I would enter the apartment, take off my shoes, and rush over to the flower pot sitting on a shelf by the window.

Light, water, minerals, dark. Soon everything assumed that simple rhythm. I would open my eyes, drink a glass of water, eat corn flakes and french fries, drop off into sleep. The cyclamen did not prosper. At first it looked as if I might be succeeding, thought I felt that, for true success, I should be speaking in the first person plural, that the cyclamen would become a part of me only if I became a part of it.

One night when I couldn't fall asleep because of the strong light of the full, silvery moon, I sat in the other chair, next to the cyclamen, and stared out into the empty street for a long while. Once, as a boy, I had believed that things will happen if you believe enough in them. I tried telling this to the cyclamen. I did not say that now I know how things happen despite our will, colluding with the will of others, perhaps, but not our own. We are mere witnesses to our own lives.

I fell asleep on the chair with my head against the sill. When I woke, I saw two wilted leaves. I raked the soil, added a few droplets of the liquid with the minerals, poured water into the little saucer under the pot. At noon I had to go out to a meeting with my adviser from the government employment agency. The agency was on the other side of town, and while I was still quite far from home, on one of the buses, I felt a momentary lapse, as if my heart had stopped for an instant or as if it bent over to peer into a newly formed void. I got off the bus and began to run.

No matter how I ran I couldn't change reality. Superman may be able to turn back the course of events and spin the world in the opposite direction, but as far as the rest of us are concerned we can only go along in the direction everything else is going in and follow the implacable sequence of day and night, waking and sleeping. When I entered the apartment—the place—the cyclamen was already done for, though it took a few more days for all the leaves and flowers to droop over the edges of the pot.

Then the snow began to fall. It fell all night and all the next day and again all that night, and in the morning when I got up it was showing no sign of letting up. I opened the window and large flakes floated into the room. One fell on the wilted cyclamen, I felt another on my face, three nestled into the yellowed carpeting.

I sat on the chair, crossed my legs, hugged my arms, closed my eyes. Under my eyelids I saw myself striding over whiteness: I was walking away leaving no trail behind. I put out my hand without opening my eyes and tried to find the edge of the chair across from me. I couldn't. I stretched out the other, again without success, and there I sat, like a blind man, while the voice from the whiteness shouted out words in languages, none of which was mine.

II

LEARNING CYRILLIC

1.

I LEAVE THE church at nine sharp. Outside it is a clear, winter night, the church steps are slippery, the cold air slices my breath. I move slowly; I grab for the frozen shrubbery. Next time, I say to myself, wear high-topped shoes. Then I spot the Indian. He is standing by a round traffic sign. He has on a leather jacket with long fringes, and he is wearing boots decorated with Indian symbols. As I am walking by him, I see his eyes are closed. "Hey," says the Indian, "what's the rush?"

2.

Fridays I go to church. I do not go to pray; I hold classes in the Serbian language for the children of emigrants. The class starts at 7:00 p.m. for the little ones aged six to nine. It ends at a quarter to eight, and the class for children between nine and sixteen begins at eight. There are no sixteen-year-olds among these kids; the oldest is a thirteen-year-old boy. There are twenty boys and girls in the first group; in the second the most I ever get are seven or eight students, but only three come regularly. One six-year-old boy stays on for the older class because his sister is in it. She, however, never comes to the class for the little ones, though their parents probably drop them off together at 7 p.m. The children in the first group like singing, while the children in the second group don't like anything. I think they hate me; I do my best to avoid looking at them.

3.

A week later, right at nine, the Indian is standing in the same place. He has on that same leather jacket with the long fringes, but this time he is wearing sneakers. And his eyes aren't closed: they gleam as he watches me walk toward him. Passing by him, I slip, stagger, and barely regain my balance. The Indian says nothing. When I turn to look back a bit later, he is still standing there. He could do with a hat, I think. The Indian raises his hand and waves.

4.

The little ones are working on their Cyrillic. I print the letters out on a smooth whiteboard with a wide, blue, felt-tip pen. Then I dictate short sentences for the practice of Cyrillic: "Лела љуља Љиљану: Lela rocks Ljiljana. Ђак носи џак: The pupil carries a sack. And Ћира има чир: Ćira has an ulcer." The children lick their lips while their pencils follow the curves of the letters. There are reproductions behind them along the whole wall of frescoes from Serbian monasteries. I count the ones where I have been, and then the ones I have never seen. I believe I saw a peacock at Ravanica, but I am not sure.

5.

During recess, while I am sipping some water in the kitchenette, I ask the priest about the peacocks. He had seen them somewhere, too, he says, but he doesn't know where. And anyway, he says, he doesn't think much of peacocks. Such a pretty bird, he adds, and such a squawking call. I try to remember the call of the peacock, but I can't pin it down. The priest asks whether I know that the peacock's tail, all those gaudy feathers, is not in fact its tail, but a kind of decorative mask with which the peacock conceals its real tail. I know nothing about peacocks, so I shrug. The peacock does not like living alone, says the priest. If its mate dies, the male flies away. Where to? I ask. Somewhere it will be loved, says the priest.

6.

You have to take a zig-zag path from the church to my house. When you leave the church and pass by the round traffic sign, you should turn right, then left into the first street, and then take the second right, and then again onto the first left. It takes about ten minutes to walk, twenty at the outside. The Indian is not standing in his place, but when I turn left, I have a sense that I can see him out of the corner of my eye. I turn. He's not there. I keep walking, now certain he's following me. I imagine mocassins on his feet, then I stop, crouch, pretend to tie my shoe, and snatch a glance over my shoulder. The street is empty. The yellow light on the stop light is blinking. When I stand back up, I feel lightheaded. I turn right, then left, I speed up as I walk and turn to look back more and more often. There is no one there. I enter the house, out of breath, lean pressing back against the door, flick on the light, cough. The parakeet watches me from its cage in the corner.

7.

The next Friday, the priest stops me at the door out of the church. He says he'd remembered where he had seen peacocks. "Where?" I ask. "At a zoo," says the priest, but then he immediately adds that he doesn't know which city the zoo was in. All he can remember is that none of the peacocks, and there were at least three males with a dozen females, wanted to stop and spread its tail. "We hopped around by the railing," said the priest, "flapped our arms, shouted all sorts of nonsense, but none of it helped. A few of them squawked is all," continued the priest, "and the call was so raucous we were doubled over laughing." "Who was?" I asked. The priest turns to the left and to the right. "Best not to get into that now," says the priest and straight off asks me whether I am pleased with how the kids are doing. I answer in the affirmative, but I complain of the shortage of books and primers, and just at that moment some members of the church's school council appear and the priest invites them to join us.

Word by word, agreement by agreement, promise by promise, I only leave the church at about 9:30. The Indian is standing next to the round traffic sign, rubbing his hands. "You were in such a rush last time," he says as I walked by him, "and now you are late: when will you make up your mind?" I take a few more steps, and then stop. I don't turn around. I am not far from him: I can hear him breathe. When the breathing stops, I keep going, across the street, between the parked cars, all the way home.

8.

While I am sitting in a restaurant, drinking coffee with milk, the Indian stands on the sidewalk across the street. Later, when I go to the supermarket, I see him over by the fruit and vegetable counter. While I stand in line at the bank, he sits in an armchair and studies the instructions for taking out a loan. At the playground, where boys and girls are chasing around in the snow after a soccer ball, I don't see him at first. Later I notice him: he is crouching behind the shrubbery.

9.

The priest comes into the room where I am holding class. The boys and girls look up from their books. The priest comes over to my desk, leans toward me and whispers in my ear. His breath is warm and smells of mint. I get up and leave with him. I stand at the door and tell the children to behave themselves. The children acquiesce, they nod, but I know they know I don't trust them. I close the door and trot after the priest, I am almost running as I enter his office. The priest is standing by the window. He beckons to me, and when I am right next to him, I see where he is looking. The Indian is standing on the path leading to the church. He is dressed in his ceremonial gear with all sorts of fringe and gaudy baubles, he is wearing moccasins, and he has an eagle feather and bison horn headdress. "I asked him what he is doing here," says the priest. "And what did he say?" I ask. "He is waiting for an answer," says the priest. "From whom?" I ask. The priest shrugs. "Maybe he meant the church," I say, "or God?" "I already asked him that," says the priest. "So what did he say?" I ask. "Nothing," says the priest. Both of us look out the window a little longer. The Indian does not move. Children's voices can be heard far off, giggling and shrieking. I tell the priest to see to the children and then I go out. My eyes smart from the cold. "It's time," says the Indian when I go over to him. He puts out his closed hand to me, then he opens it slowly. I don't see anything in his hand, but I know what is there. The Indian turns and leaves, and I go back to the church. I find the priest sitting on the desk, reading the children a poem by the poet Uncle Jova Zmaj. One of the little girls has put her head down on her desk and fallen asleep. When the priest turns the page, she opens her eyes.

10.

I am not surprised when I see that the Indian is waiting for me out in front of my house. The day is bright, sunny and the cold air only nips at the face. The Indian is a head taller than I am. When he offers me his hand, my hand is swallowed by his fist.

11.

We sit in the front room of the City Museum, near the door that leads to an exhibit dedicated to the Blackfoot tribe. "The Siksika," says the Indian, "not the Blackfeet." "White people talk about the Blackfeet," he adds, "but the real people speak only of the Siksika." "You are a Siksika?" I ask. The Indian says yes, he is. "Maybe now," I continue, "you can tell me your name." "Maybe," says the Indian; then he says nothing. After a while, right as the woman at the cash register yawns, the Indian says, "Thunder Cloud."

12.

Thunder Cloud is patient. While I look at the paintings and objects, he leafs through the catalogue. Now and then he comes over and peers over my shoulder. When one of the captions gives a word in his language, he says it a few times. Then he urges me to say it, but when I finally do, he clicks his tongue and shakes his head.

13.

"I saw you yesterday with the Indian," says a blond-haired boy. The other children stop writing. "I once had my picture taken with an Indian at a rodeo," says a little girl with her hair in pigtails. For a moment we all look at her. "The sun was so hot," says the little girl, "that I had to wear dark glasses." "His Indian," says the blond-haired boy, "is at least six feet tall." Now they are all looking at me. "Today we are going to read a new story," I say. I pick up a black, felt-tip pen and write at the top of the board: "The Dark Land."

14.

The priest is vexed. Ever since the Indian has started standing in front of the church, women have been complaining and saying they fear for their safety. "Yesterday," says the priest, "Mrs. Vidosava was here, the one who has that fur coat, and she said she shakes from head to foot whenever she thinks of that Indian, and when she sees him her knees knock and her heart jumps to her throat. She showed me," said the priest, "how she shakes." The priest spreads his arms and legs, rolls back his eyes, sticks out his tongue, and shakes. "Something along those lines," he says when he stops, "though she is better at it than I am." "But," I reply, "Thunder Cloud is not dangerous. I am sure he'd never even trod on an ant. And besides," I add, "he has no interest in white women." The priest looks at me suspiciously and asks how I know. "I know," I say, "because he is a traditional Indian and the only thing that matters to him is preserving the purest possible legacy for his tribe." "What tribe?" asks the priest. "The Siksika," I say. "Who are they?" asks the priest. "They used to be called the Blackfeet," I say. "Didn't there used to be a comic strip," muses the priest, "back in Serbia, with Indians from that tribe?" I know nothing about a comic strip, so I keep my mouth shut. The priest scratches his neck and behind his ears. "First the Indians killed some newcomers and took their children into slavery," says the priest, "and then the English soldiers came, or was it the French, and killed all the Indians, but they didn't find the children... or did they find them after all? I don't remember," says the priest, "but one of the Indians was a Blackfoot, I'm sure of it."

15.

"My father died from drink," says Thunder Cloud, "my mother died from drink, my brother died from drink, my sister died from drink." He looks at me, "Who died from drink in your family?" "No one," I say.

16.

It is cold, but the Indian is standing by the round traffic sign and he is not moving. "How much longer can he keep that up?" asks the priest. "Until morning," I answer. We are standing in front of the window, partially hidden by the curtain. We watch an elderly woman, short and wearing a hat, as she comes up to the street corner. When she gets to the Indian, she stops and looks him up and down. Her eyes travel slowly, as if she wants to see, maybe even commit to memory, every single spangle, every shred of fringe, every bead and every feather. The Indian stands and doesn't breathe. "He has to breathe," says the priest, "there is no living being that can last with no oxygen." The woman says something and the Indian leans over the better to hear her. Then he flings back his head and laughs. He guffaws, everything reverberates, and the old woman taps her foot merrily all the while. White fluffy snow wafts up into the air.

17.

There are only four children this evening in the second group, counting the six-year-old boy who is here with his older sister. None of them says anything, and since I'm not asking, we sit there, silent; various sounds reach us. The thumping from the floor below is from members of the folklore group practicing the steps of circle dances. A restrained murmur, somewhere from beneath our feet, comes from the banter of the parents who wait in the room by the bar for the kids working on their Serbian language and folkdances. Marica is at the bar, and on the board behind her is a list of all the available items: beer, hot brandy, juices and sandwiches. Unfortunately, there are no pastries. There are times when the parents regret that the lessons finish so soon, and that they can't stay longer, to have at least one more beer. I watch my little group and wonder who will be the first to speak. Then music can be heard downstairs, and then the thumping in search of the rhythm. I tap the rough surface of the table. "I hate that music," says the girl to her little brother. My finger freezes mid-air. Her brother giggles.

18.

When we get closer to the panel with the large photograph of an Indian chief, Thunder Cloud says: "My great grandfather." I look at the picture, I look at Thunder Cloud: the prominent, highly raised cheekbones are the same, the narrow, crooked nose, the deeply set lines that run from the nostrils to the corners of the mouth. It says below the picture: An unknown Indian chief, the Siksika tribe, circa 1860 (?). I draw Thunder Cloud's attention to the caption. Thunder Cloud snorts derisively. "If there's something a white man doesn't know," he says, "does that mean no one knows it?" "Absolutely not," I say. "Don't you think I'd know my own great grandfather?" says Thunder Cloud. "Of course," I reply. "His name was Black Otter," says Thunder Cloud. "Black Otter," I repeat. "One night," continues Thunder Cloud, "he dreamed he was battling a group of Shoshones, and when he faced the fact that he would be unable to fend them off any more, he leaped into a river, where, instead of drowning, he turned into an otter. When he woke up, he was wet from head to toe. He left the tent and said to his mother, 'I am Black Otter.' 'Fine,' said his mother, 'but first get out of those wet clothes.' 'I will draw an otter on our tent first,' he said, and then he sketched a black otter on the four sides of the tent, so it could protect them from every danger, no matter which direction the danger was coming from. Then he drew circles that were the stars in the night sky, a little cross that was a moth that brought good dreams, a wriggly line that was the hilly countryside where they lived. His mother waited patiently all that time, holding dry clothes. Black Otter put down the paint and changed his clothes, and a little later a photographer just happened to turn up." "And this is the picture?" I ask. "This is it," says Thunder Cloud.

19.

"And now," I say, as I finish reading the story, "any questions?" The girl with the pigtails raises her hand, "Why," she asks, "do they call the Indians Blackfeet?" "Because they don't wash their feet," says the boy sitting in the front row. I wait for the giggles to subside, and then I say, "That's not used for all Indians, only for the ones who belong to the Blackfoot tribe, and they got the name, which is 'Siksika' in their language. It was given to them because an ancestor of theirs had moccasins that turned black after he walked over land that had burned in a prairie fire." No one is listening any more.

20.

Thunder Cloud and I are sitting together at a library. There is a pile of books in front of us about the Indians of North America. Thunder Cloud shows me a photograph of Crowfoot, the greatest chief of the Siksikas, and Crowfoot's family. In it we see Crowfoot, a woman, probably his wife, and eight children. The photograph was taken in 1884, says the caption, and over the next six years almost all of them died of tuberculosis and other diseases, including Crowfoot. I imagine all those plagues, all those quick and slow deaths, words sputtered in delirium, the loss of hope, the absence of comfort, the vast prairie that suddenly has no shelter to offer anymore. "You could mount the fastest horse and ride it until it dropped from exhaustion," says Thunder Cloud, "and still you couldn't outrun the sickness. And that," he says, "was the most awful plague the white man brought with him, that kind of killing both near and far, when he was there and even when he wasn't. We weren't afraid of death," says Thunder Cloud, "but what we meant by that was an honorable death, a death in battle or from wounds, or old age, when the body goes back to its maker, and now we had to face a kind of death that killed for the sake of killing, as if enjoying it." Thunder Cloud stops talking, sets the palms of his hands on the table. Snow is falling outside.

21.

"Who knows," says the priest, "what he believes in, and whether he believes in anything?" Thunder Cloud laughs when I translate the priest's question for him. He laughs for a long time, his head flung back, till tears come to his eyes. Then he asks the priest what the priest believes. "In a community of freedom between God and man through Jesus Christ," says the priest. "What does that mean?" asks Thunder Cloud when I translate the priest's words for him into English. "A community of freedom is a community of love," answers the priest, "because without love there can be no faith." Thunder Cloud considers this for a time. "So," he says, "you love to be free?" "No," says the priest, "first you have to become free, and only after that can you begin to love." "And before that," asks Thunder Cloud, "could it be that before that there is no love?" "Love is not an emotion," says the priest, "love is community with another person." "So that means," Thunder Cloud glowered over him, "that you can be with another person you don't love, but that still counts as love?" The priest huffs.

"I have a headache," he says. "Me, too," says Thunder Cloud. "I could do with a strong cup of coffee," says the priest. "Me too," says Thunder Cloud. "Marica," calls the priest, "please bring us two cups of Turkish coffee!"

22.

Thunder Cloud sits in a chair and watches the kids. The kids watch Thunder Cloud. "What's this now?" I break the silence, "isn't there anyone with a question for our guest?" The girl with the pigtails raises her hand, "Does he know Serbian?" "He does not," I say, "he is an Indian." "Some Indians know Serbian," speaks up a boy who is sitting at the back of the room. "How do you know?" asks the boy sitting next to him. "My father said so," says the first boy. Thunder Cloud doesn't move. From where I'm standing, right by the door, it looks as if he isn't breathing at all. "Your father doesn't know from shit," says the other boy, "Indians speak only English." "They speak their own languages, too," I interrupt. Then I ask Thunder Cloud to say something in his language. Thunder Cloud says a short sentence in which consonants and vowels follow in rapid succession. "What is he saying?" asks the girl from the first row. "I was telling," says Thunder Cloud, "how the moon and a wolf meet every summer night on a hill by Yellow River." "How do you say 'wolf'?" asks the little girl. "Makoiyi," says Thunder Cloud. "And 'moon'?" "Kokomikisomm," says Thunder Cloud. "And 'summer'?" "Niipo," says Thunder Cloud. The little girl with the pigtails raises her hand again: "May I ask him something in English?" I nod. The girl gets up, coughs, and asks, "Why do Indians live in those round, tall tents, and not in a house?" "Because," answers Thunder Cloud, "the devil can chase you into the corner of a house, but in our tent, that we call a tipi, there are no corners, so the devil stays away." "OK," says the little girl, and sits down. The parents start appearing at the door. "Practice your Cyrillic," I say to the kids, "next week we'll have a test."

23.

The jangling of the phone wakes me up in the middle of the night. I poke around on the bedside table, knock a book to the floor, the alarm clock flies after it, but I do find the receiver and pull it to my ear. "I can't sleep," says the priest. "What's up?" I ask. "I don't know," says the priest, "maybe it's the full moon." I looked out the window: the moon is, indeed, full and is suspended above the city like a bloated squash. I ask the priest whether he has drawn the curtains. "I have," says the priest. Had he had a cup of mint tea? Yes, he had. Had he counted sheep? Yes, but in vain. Had he tried thinking of nothing? "What do you mean, of nothing?" asks the priest. "You need to focus," I say, "and breathe carefully until your mind is all empty." "Is this Eastern heresy?" asks the priest. "That depends," I say. "Then it is," answers the priest, "and in that case I would rather stay awake." I shrug. "Good night," says the priest. "Good night."

24.

We stop by a photograph of an Indian woman drying meat. "The dried meat was mixed with dried berries," says Thunder Cloud. Bison fat was added to it, and this mixture, called *mokimaani*, was the staple during wintertime. Wrapped up in blankets, with kerchiefs tied around their heads, the Indian women did not look noble the way the men did. "You are wrong," says Thunder Cloud, "the women of the Blackfoot tribe were as powerful as the men. The tipi belonged to the woman," he says, "because the woman built it and kept it, and if she wanted to separate from a man she had been living with until then, all she had to do was to leave his things out in front in a pile." "And what would he do then?" I ask. "He would look to find himself another woman," says Thunder Cloud, "and another tent." I imagine an Indian moving around among the tipis early in the morning. His arms are full of his things, some of them roll off and drop to the ground, but he isn't able to pick them up. The tipis stand so their entrances face eastward. The sun comes slowly up on the edge of the prairie, the entrance to the tipi opens and the morning prayers move skyward. "If I keep walking like this," thinks that Indian, "I will leave the camp and I won't stop before Milk River." Then a hand appears at the entrance to a tent and beckons. The Indian stops, puts his things down, and waves back. The hand waves to him once more, and then disappears. The Indian lifts his things, not noticing a string of beads that stays in the damp grass, and walks over to the tent. I will bring my horse over later, he thinks as he gets to the entrance. Then he steps into the gloom.

25.

The kids who come to the church, regardless of age, speak only Serbian with me. The minute they stop talking to me and turn to talk to each other they switch to English. It is enough for me to turn my back for a moment to start writing something on the board or to look for something among the books and papers, and the room where we work is filled with English words. "But, why?" I ask them, "How can it be that you are unable to speak with your friends in your native language?" They look at me, say nothing, blink. "Come on," I say to the boy with the curly hair, "ask your friend something, but in Serbian!" "He is not my friend," says the boy with the curly hair. "Ask him something anyway," I say. The boy with the curly hair stares at the boy next to him. "How are you," he finally says, in Serbian. "I am fine," says the other boy, also in Serbian. Both of them look up at me, as proud as if they had been reciting *Hamlet*. "Now you ask him something," I tell the other boy. The other boy stares at the boy with the curly hair. "And how are you?" he says, finally. "Not bad," says the boy with the curly hair. Again the two of them turn to me. "Excellent," I say. "Should I try something else?" asks the other boy. I look at my watch: quarter to eight. "Next Friday," I say, "and for your homework, write out a conversation with your best friend in Cyrillic." "My best friend is in Osijek," says a little girl with bangs "Imagine that she is here," I say, "that she has come to visit you and that you are telling her about the things she will be seeing." "She will never come here," says the little girl with bangs. "Maybe you will go there," I say. "I'll ask my mother," says the girl with bangs, gets up and goes out with the other kids. They are speaking English, of course, but whispering.

26.

When I leave the church, the snow squeaks under foot, puffs of breath rise and disperse above. For the first time in four weeks Thunder Cloud is not standing by the round traffic sign. I lean over, and, just in case, I kneel and search for footprints, but the snow around the sign has not been tamped down. I carefully brush away the top layer of snow: perhaps someone was standing here before and then left, for whatever reason, and then new snow fell and covered the older footprints, but no matter how deep I dig, I find nothing. The concrete sidewalk surface soon appears and I feel my fingers freeze. I start to put back the snow, fill the hole carefully, and then I understand the pointlessness of what I am doing, I straighten up suddenly and stomp on the snow all around the metal pole that the round traffic sign is attached to. The blood rushes to my head, and I get dizzy and feel I might keel over. I grab the pole and let it go just as fast, because my fingers burn from the cold. I stagger, take a step or two back, and all around me patches of light shimmer in the air. "Breathe deeply," I say to myself, then I take a deep breath, hold it and count to ten and then I let it out slowly through my nose. The flashing lights stop, night comes back, the round traffic sign is where it always was. Someone had tamped down all the snow around, but new snow is starting to fall, and quickly, faster than anyone can imagine, it will look just as it had a few minutes ago, unblemished and smooth, like a secret.

27.

"If a wife is unfaithful," says Thunder Cloud, "they cut her nose off."
I cringe as I look at the photograph of an Indian woman with no
nose. "Why," I ask, "do they cut off the nose?" Thunder Cloud looks
over at me. "And what else," he asks and shakes his head, "could
they cut off?" "I don't know," I answer, "fingers, perhaps? An ear?"
Thunder Cloud sighs, he has probably had just about had it with
these ignorant white people who want everything explained to them.
"When you cut off a woman's ear," he says, "she can hide the wound
or scar under her hair or a kerchief; if you cut off her fingers, then
she is useless; but if you cut off her nose, then everyone can see what
she has done and it will never occur to her to cheat on her husband
again." The Indian woman in the photograph is staring straight at
the camera and she does not look chagrined. "What did they do with
the nose?" I ask. Thunder Cloud shrugs. "Well they didn't drop it on
the ground," I say, "for the dogs." I picture a scrawny, spotted dog
carrying a nose in its muzzle racing among the tents while after it,
barking furiously, scampers a pack of other dogs and little children.
"Did they keep it," I ask, "as a totem against curses?" "They buried
it, maybe" Thunder Cloud replies, "so no one could ever find it, people or dogs." That I can see, I think, a little burial ground with tiny
mounds, where someone, despite the secrecy, leaves a fragrant wild
flower now and then. The sun slowly sets over the edge of the prairie,
the shadows get longer, dark creeps down the stems, and then all is
dark. The leaves rustle when the wind blows and that is all.

28.

My eyes snap open, but there is no one at the window. My eyes shut,
and then open again. Nothing happens. I must have been dreaming,
because just a moment earlier, I am sure of it, by the lower right-
hand corner of the window frame, I saw Thunder Cloud's face. He
was shading his eyes with his right hand as if he were trying to see better
into the room, to spot me in the shadows. His lips were moving but you

couldn't hear anything. He had two feathers in his hair, both of them white with black tips. A thick shock of hair smeared with grease and cut straight across, falls over his forehead. Drops of liquid appear on the windowpane, making a white circle, and Thunder Cloud collects them on the tip of his tongue now and then, as if he were licking ice cream. I could get up now and go over to the window, and see whether the corner of the pane is smudged, but I don't move. Sometimes it is better to do nothing.

29.

After class, while I sort through my papers and books, a woman wearing a long coat comes over. It turns out she is the mother of the little girl with the pigtails. "How is my girl doing?" asks the woman. "Is she keeping up with her assignments?" I answer that she's fine, but that she isn't doing every homework assignment, which isn't so bad, I add, because this is not obligatory schooling, it is an extra class. "She has to study," says the woman. "Otherwise how will she go back if she doesn't even know her own language?" I nod, push the books into a drawer, put my papers into a plastic bag. I notice the woman watching everything I do. "Those are their assignments," I say. "Tonight I have to go over them and grade them." Now the woman nods. "I, too, used to work with kids," she says, "but littler ones, at a nursery school." I don't know what to say to that. I say nothing and listen to the crinkling of the plastic bag. "I wanted to ask you something," says the woman, "but perhaps this isn't the best moment." I look at her. She has blue eyes. The woman suffers my gaze, and then raises her hand and touches her fingers to her neck. "Don't," she says, "we are in a church, after all."

30.

"Another unfaithful woman," says Thunder Cloud, "whose nose was cut off. Not her whole nose," he adds when he sees the shadow of horror on my face, "but the tip of her nose, just enough so that everyone can see she was unfaithful." He pushes an open book across the table, moves it toward me until it touches my fingertips. The image is fuzzy and it is hard to see the disfigured nose. It is easy to see, however, that the woman is squinting, perhaps from the sun, or maybe because she feels awkward. Her squinting eyelids and the lifted corners of her mouth form the impression that the woman is about to cry, that she is on the verge of tears. She is wearing a necklace with two strings of beads. The picture is black and white, but I assume the two strings of the necklace were in different colors. The hair is definitely dark, parted in the middle, and tied in braids thrown back behind her. "Sometimes the braids," says Thunder Cloud, "went halfway down the back, or to the waist, or even further." I hand him back the book. I push it across the table back the other way, until it touches his fingertips. "What are you thinking," asks Thunder Cloud, "whether it hurts when they cut off your nose?"

31.

Thunder Cloud and I go to a saint's day party. While we are on our way to the northern part of town on a bus, I explain to him what a saint's day party is about, and how you are supposed to act at one. Ever since I've known him, ever since he entered, in the literal sense of the word, my life, this is the first time he is nervous. He asks me three times how his new leather jacket looks, are the fringes tidy, whether the beads are tangled, whether his part is straight. I tell him not to worry, that he has never looked better. "You should have seen me ten years ago," says Thunder Cloud. "You should have seen *me* ten years ago," I reply. "The whole world was way better ten years ago," says Thunder Cloud. Except for him and me the only other person on the bus is an old woman. She is sitting in front of us and turns around to look at us from time to time. The bus driver looks at us, too, not directly, but in the rearview mirror. Thunder Cloud pays no attention to them. "Maybe I should have brought my tobacco and other things with me, so that I could smoke a peace pipe with the host." I imagine the priest, pipe in hand, his cheeks puffed with biting smoke. "Next time we smoke the peace pipe," I say to Thunder Cloud. "Now we will eat sweet, cooked wheat and drink brandy." "I don't like brandy," says Thunder Cloud. "You needn't drink it down," I say. "It'll do to lick the rim of the glass." Thunder Cloud turns to look out the window. The driver's eyes appear again in the rearview mirror. The old woman coughs. The bus stops, the front door opens, a group of teenagers tumbles in with cries and laughter. The boys are wearing wide, baggy pants; the girls despite the cold, have short tops on that don't even cover their midriffs; they have locks of hair dyed in all different colors. They drop into the seats as if they'd been doing hard labor until then, put their feet up, lean their heads back on the windowpane, rub their eyes. Then they all start talking at once, even the old woman; leaning forward, she starts telling the driver something. The driver answers, but the woman doesn't hear, and she props a hand behind her ear. A little later, everyone stops talking.

32.

"Adam, the first man, refused to enter into a community with God," says the priest, "and so it was that though it looked as if he were winning freedom, in fact he was embracing death. And he wasn't just embracing death for his own sake," continued the priest, "but for all of nature. All of nature," says the priest and spreads his hands, "is mortal thanks to Adam's choice. Because with his denial Adam was preventing nature from overcoming its own mortality. But God is good," smiled the priest, "and instead of turning his back on man and consigning him completely to oblivion, he created a community through his son, Jesus Christ, who became a man and thereby made it possible for nature and people to achieve immortality in community with him." Thunder Cloud waits patiently for me to finish my stuttering translation of the priest's words, and then he says, "I know a different story. This is how it was: one day Napi, whom you call the Old Man, fashioned the world from mud, including a woman for himself. Napi and his wife made people, but they couldn't agree on everything. Napi, for instance, wanted people to have ten fingers on each hand, but his wife felt it would be better for them to have four fingers and a thumb, and that it is how it was in the end. One of the things they could not agree on was death. They argued, and argued, and then Napi said, 'I will throw a piece of bison manure into the water; if it floats on the surface then man will be dead for four days and then come back to life again. If it sinks, then he will die for good.' He tossed a little chunk of bison manure into water and it floated. His wife, however, objected. She said, 'Manure is no good for these things; I will toss this stone into the water; if it floats on the surface, people will be dead for four days and then come back to life again, and if it sinks, they will die for good.' The stone sank, and death arrived among people, but Napi and his wife weren't sorry, because if people had lived forever, then they would never have felt compassion for those near to them." Now it is the priest waiting patiently for me to finish my jerky translation of the Indian's words, and while he listens, he shakes his head from time to time. "The mud is the same as it is in our story," says the priest in the end, "and their death, too, is eternal because they do not embrace a community with God, though it isn't easy to decide between a piece of bison manure and a piece of stone." "Should I translate that for him?" I ask. "No need," says the priest. He takes Thunder Cloud's hand in his and slowly enunciates, word for word, in Serbian, "The doors to eternal life open through God, do you understand?" Thunder Cloud nods and grins. "Hallelujah!" he says, "hallelujah!" Then he turns to me. "I should have brought the peace pipe," he says.

33.

The kids sitting at the first desk slide over and make room for Thunder Cloud. Squeezed between them, Thunder Cloud looks like a giant. "I am Vladimir," says the boy sitting to his right. "And I'm Ružica," says the girl sitting to his left. "I'm Thunder Cloud," says Thunder Cloud. "We know," answer the children in a chorus. "Who," I ask, "is going to show our guest Cyrillic?" They all raise their hands, some stand up, one boy climbs up onto his chair, another leans on the Indian's back. Thunder Cloud also raises his hand, trying to calm them, and when he sees that they are paying no attention, he throws his head back and lets out a long, trembling cry. They all stop talking. Thunder Cloud grins. "That is part of a song," he says, "that we used to sing before we scalped our enemy after we conquered him." "What does it mean, to scalp," asks Vladimir. "That's when you chop someone's hair off their head," says a boy in a striped shirt, "but along with the skin." "Ow, that hurts," says Ružica. "It doesn't hurt," says Thunder Cloud, "because the enemy is usually dead before that." "Who killed him?" asks Vladimir. "Our guest has come for us to show him Cyrillic," I say, "and not to discuss the art of warfare." "Maybe next time he can bring a tomahawk," says the boy in the striped shirt. "OK," I reply, "and now why doesn't someone write out a sentence using Cyrillic letters on the board." No one moves. "They don't have to write anything," says Thunder Cloud, "why don't they tell me a story about Cyrillic letters." "What sort of story?" I ask. "When we want to learn about a thing," says Thunder Cloud, "they tell us the story of how it came into the world. Everything has its own story," he says, "every living and non-living thing, and when you know its story, then you know the thing the story is about." "Yeah," pipes up Vladimir, "so how did Cyrillic begin?" "Once, in the olden days," I say, "many, many years ago, there was a man on the muddy shore of a lake who saw the tracks of marsh birds and thought that these tracks, which told him which birds were here and what they were doing, could be used for writing down other things, too. He took a stick," I go on, "and on the soft earth he first wrote the letter A; later he made up the rest of the letters, the period, comma, exclamation point and question mark, and that is how Cyrillic first began." "I didn't know that," says the boy in the striped shirt. "Me neither," says Vladimir. "Me neither," said Ružica. They all look at Thunder Cloud. "Were those the tracks of a heron?" he asks.

34.

The phone rings late at night. "What's this about a heron?" shouts the priest, "what is this nonsense, what is he going on about?" I hold the receiver away from my ear, and then bring it back as the priest's voice dies down. "He didn't say that the heron invented Cyrillic," I repeat. "It was me telling a story about how Cyrillic came from the tracks of birds on the shore of a lake, and that is when he brought up the heron." There was silence at the other end of the line. "Hello?" I say. "What lake?" asks the priest. "Excuse me?" "Where was the lake," asks the priest. "I don't know," I say, "maybe Ohrid?" "Do herons live there?" asks the priest. "There must be birds," I say, "I wouldn't be surprised if there were a heron." The priest coughs. "I was worried sick," he says, "now I feel better." "Me, too," I say. "Good night," says the priest. "Good night," I say and hang up the phone. A moment later the phone rings again. "It's me," says the priest. "I know," I reply. "Do you have any idea," asks the priest, "what a heron looks like?"

35.

The first of the rooms, the smaller, has displays on the earliest North American Indians. Then you go into the next, slightly larger room, dedicated to the history of the Blackfoot tribe. That room leads into a third, the largest hall, brightly lit, which is full of displays and scenes from everyday life, including a tall tent, a tipi, raised in the middle of the room. We go over slowly, as if we are creeping up on it. There are deer drawn on the tent. Their hoofs rest on a wavy line that goes around the whole tent, while their horns are touching black circles. "Those are stars," says Thunder Cloud, "and the lines are mountain rivers, so that the one who lives in this tipi is valiant as a deer on a cliff and will not stop until he touches the stars." One of the tent flaps is raised and, when I peer in, I can see clothing hanging on a string, a bed covered in blankets, two pairs of moccasins, an empty kettle, a bow and a quiver. "Come in," says Thunder Cloud, and touches my shoulder with the tips of his fingers. I bend over, take a step, enter, and straighten up. I hear Thunder Cloud lowering the tent flap. For a moment I'm frightened: nothing easier than getting lost where no one gets lost. The light in the tent is gentle, thick, almost milky, and when I turn to the middle, it seems to be following me, as if I am entering a cocoon of glow. I look up and through the opening at the top of the tent I see the stars. It is night. A coyote howls, then an owl hoots, then everything is still. Then a branch snaps under someone's foot and fear creeps into my throat, my forehead beads with sweat. I drop to my knees, lie on my side. The stars move faster and faster across the rim of the opening, leaving a pale trail behind them. I shut my eyes and I'm gone.

36.

Someone taps softly and persistently at my window, but I do not get up. I pull my head under the covers, curl into a ball, press my ears with my hands. When I drag myself out of bed in the morning, there is nothing to see, and there are no footprints in the snow. I look into the mailbox, just in case someone has put a message in there for me, but the mailbox is empty. I walk all the way around the house, peer into the garage, poke a finger into the little birdhouse: nothing has changed. Only later, under a bush, I find a dead mouse.

37.

On Friday, exactly at nine, I leave the church. There is a warm wind blowing and the snow is melting under foot. A fire truck siren howls in the 104 distance. When I pass by the round traffic sign, it creaks as if it is remembering something. I think of stopping, of inspecting it up close, but I know the priest is standing at the window, behind the curtain, and that he is watching me. I don't stop, I keep going, all the way to the crosswalk. I wait for the light to change, and when the green letters invite me to walk, I start to walk until I find myself across the street.

FROM THE spot where he stood, on the highest platform of the ski jump at Lahti, a man in a black suit jacket could see a young woman on a path leading toward the entrance and the ski lifts. From that height she seemed short and plump, but when she got off the lift and came over to the railing, he realized he'd been mistaken yet again: the young woman was thin and almost a head taller than he. He had been wrong the day before, too, when he had believed, at breakfast in the hotel, that the woman with her back to him at a table nearby was elderly and frail. When she got up and walked over to the door to leave, she turned out to be young and several months pregnant. Maybe the time has come, he thought at that point, to stop this game, but when he found himself up on top of the ski lift and saw the young woman, who was now leaning gingerly on the railing, he had to have another go. Without success, of course, but he knew that to start with.

He couldn't remember how he started playing this guessing game, as he called it, for himself. The game must have occurred to him when he saw that Elizabeta was serious about them stopping seeing each other. While she was saying what she had to say, and had obviously rehearsed, she turned her back to him and stared out the window into the messy yard. From this came the simple game: whenever he caught sight of a woman with her back turned, he would try to guess what she looked like. He soon saw that a person's back sends an entirely different message from the face and front of the body, and that it is nearly impossible, in fact, to predict with any certainty what any woman looks like by her back. A back that seemed broad and strong, which would have led him to expect a broad, large person in front, would hide a petite woman, with small breasts and a gaunt face, while a slightly hunched back and twisted shoulders belonged to a tall girl, with long legs and slanted eyes.

He didn't know what to do even when he got it right—though that seldom happened. He could have gone up to those women and told them that, seeing them from behind, he had guessed how they looked from the front, but that sounded silly, as if he were looking for an excuse to strike up a conversation with them, but mostly they were of no interest to him. So instead he took his pleasure in the little thrill of triumph that he allowed himself then. This is also how he worked to ease the great feeling of defeat that filled him when Elizabeta told him everything she had to say: she stopped talking, went on staring out the window, turning only some fifteen minutes later and was amazed at him still standing there. She asked him what he was doing there, and he merely shrugged. "You are crazy," said Elizabeta, "you really are crazy."

Maybe I really am crazy, thought the man as he stole glances at the tall woman. The guessing game had taken hold, and soon he was playing it for every single female figure he couldn't see clearly, either because of how far she was from him or for any other reason. On the street, in public transportation, at the train station or the airport, he did nothing else but keep an eye out for all the women he couldn't see clearly, and those who offered him the solace of their back. In the evening, as he lay in bed, the scenes that had taken shape that day paraded before him while his eyes were closed: he saw himself pushing his way through an overcrowded bus just to see the face of a woman whose back he had been watching during the ride; he saw himself striding through a park to catch up with a woman for whom, probably because of the swaying shadows of the leaves, he had been sure was dark in complexion; he lost his patience when he saw himself wait outside a boutique for a girl to come out who, he believed, based on her narrow back, had blue eyes and small teeth. And though he almost never guessed right, he was always starting over again, as if in the ritual of guessing and later admitting defeat, he found the strength to carry on.

As far as that was concerned, the young woman who was leaning on the railing was no different from the others. As usual, he hadn't guessed at all what she looked like so the game was over, but for the first time, unlike his usual distance after a defeat, he found himself standing by the object of the game. Without turning his head he tried to see her better, but the young woman straightened up, moved away from the railing, and slipped out of his field of vision. The man then straightened up, pushed off with his hands and turned. The young woman was standing at the corner of the platform, struggling to light a cigarette, but the wind was gusting, and no matter which way she turned, the flame of her lighter was blown out.

"Maybe I can help," said the man in English, he went over and spread open his suit jacket. For a moment he felt like a flasher and blushed.

The young woman didn't answer. She bowed her head and flicked the lighter. She inhaled the first smoke so long and so deeply that the man felt out of breath and had to lower his arms. The young woman didn't move, she released a cloud of smoke, still bowed over as if she wanted to bring her ear to his lips. If she had done that, wondered the man, what would he have said to her? The young woman went back to the railing and gazed out at the cityscape. She inhaled one more lungful of smoke, brought the cigarette to her nose, shuddered, and threw it away.

The man leaned over the railing to keep a better eye on the cigarette as it fell. Soon he couldn't see it, but he kept looking after it, imagining it as it struck the concrete pillars of the ski jump, the blazing sparks flying in all directions. When he straightened up, the young woman was watching him. He smiled, but her face remained serious.

Then she asked him where he was from. "Not from Lahti," she said, "because if you were, we would be speaking in Finnish rather than English."

"Yes," said the main, "I am not from Lahti." He didn't want to say any more, though he thought he would like to tell her of his whole life and wondered how long that story would take. How many sentences were necessary to sum up someone's whole life?

The young woman no longer took her eyes off him. Then she asked him for the sign he was born under.

The man asked, "Does it matter?"

"There is nothing more important in the world," answered the young woman.

"I am a Libra," said the man. He wasn't a Libra, but that seemed easier than saying he was a Virgo.

The young woman squinted a little and looked at him through her lashes. "Are you sure?" she asked finally. "You don't look like a Libra."

The man said nothing. If he had gotten snared by a lie, he didn't want to get entangled.

Somewhere behind his back the ski lift started up. Soon there were the sounds of voices and people climbing the steps. The man thought it would be good to hide, but he couldn't see anything to hide behind. The young woman kept watching him, and not once, if he had kept careful track, did she blink. Then she put out her hand to him. "Come," she said, and the man came over, stood in front of her and looked up to see her face. "Something happened to you," said the young woman, "I just don't know what." She put the palm of her right hand on his chest and the man suddenly felt that the loud beating of his heart was audible to her. "What are you," he asked in a hoarse voice, "a cardiologist?"

The young woman smiled for the first time since she'd climbed up to the top of the ski jump. "No," she said, "that I'm not, but I do know a thing or two about the human heart."

She lifted her hand and brought it, cupped, to her face as if she wanted to sniff or sip the man's heart. The man watched her movement closely, frightened at the thought that his heart might vanish before his very eyes. On his chest, on the spot where her hand had rested, he felt a mild itch, like from the healing of a wound.

"You meant to jump," said the young woman.

"No," said the man, "I did not." Then he thought he was not speaking truthfully and that only now had he really understood why he had come up to the top of the ski jump. He reached out, took hold of the young woman's cupped hand and drew it to him. It was empty.

"Do you want us to jump together," asked the young woman, "holding hands?"

The man closed his eyes. He could see how the young woman and he dropped through the air, but he did not wait to see the end of the fall. He opened his eyes and looked at the sky.

"You won't find anything up there to help you," said the young woman.

"And you?" asked the man. "Can you help me?"

The young woman crossed her hands on her chest. "I thought I already was," she said.

The man leaned on the railing again. Down there at the foot of the ski jump, he saw two women, but he did not wonder what they looked like. He looked at the young woman and in her eyes he saw tears. It's all from the wind, thought the man, there can be no other explanation. He sought the young woman's hands and squeezed them firmly. He thought of something else: regardless of the number of sentences, he wanted to tell her his whole life, from the earliest day until now, without skipping a thing, with no breaks, until he got to the place where he now stood. "Let's go," he said then to the young woman.

"Let's," said the young woman.

The man asked, "Which way?" His voice was hoarse again.

"Doesn't matter."

The man turned. Wherever he looked, in any direction, it was all the same. He gestured toward the horizon. "We're going there," he said.

"Off we go," said the young woman.

They didn't go immediately. For a time they looked at each other in silence, and once they abruptly began to move, they did not stop.

STAMPS

IN SPITE OF computers and email, Stojan Zec went on writing his letters longhand, and after he tucked each one into its envelope and inscribed the address of the recipient on it he would bring it to the post office to be weighed. The woman who worked behind the counter at the post office would put it on the scales, check the rate in the postage listings, and then—as she had countless times before—she'd leaf through her big book in search of the nicer stamps. Stojan Zec could no longer remember how long he had been bringing his letters to her; the building of the post office had last been remodeled some twenty years back but he was sure he remembered what it had looked like before, when the postal clerks had been separated from the customers by glass partitions; the middle section of the partition was made of opaque glass, so that the clerk could only be seen if Stojan Zec hunched over to speak through the opening below, or if he stood on tiptoe and peered over the top of the milky section. Even after the post office was remodeled and when, after lengthy construction, the counters were opened, in the literal sense of the word, with the removal of the partitions and that little opening or window, Stojan Zec still hadn't shed the habit of hunching over when he presented his letters, just as he couldn't stop himself, especially when the line was long, from rising up on tiptoe, which long ago, in the days of opaque glass, had been the only way to see at least something of the reason for the wait. What had surprised Stojan Zec the most, back then, however, twenty years ago, was the postal clerk's face. She had seemed, from below or above, in the abbreviated perspective, unappealing, unsightly really; but once her face was on a level with his she had an unexpectedly harmonious appearance, calm and benign, crisscrossed with alluring shadows and suggestions, especially when her hair was combed back, drawn back behind the ears or done up in a ponytail. Even today, after all these years and despite the web of thin and thick wrinkles around the corners of her eyes and ears, the expression on the face of the clerk aroused the same feeling of a pleasant stirring in Stojan Zec's chest, a stirring which, he noted, was growing weaker, but which never entirely disappeared even when her face, as now, was caught in the ghostly gleam of the monitor, like a sentinel at the gateway to a new, despised world.

Nemanja, his son, teased him mercilessly. Not, of course, for the postal clerk's face, about which he knew nothing—as, indeed, Stojan Zec knew nothing about the postal clerk—but for Stojan Zec's distrust of technological advances, his reluctance to give up outmoded tools (the fountain pen, the typewriter, carbon paper, erasers), and his unwillingness to learn at least the essential operations needed for use of the computer. "Today everyone," Nemanja said, "absolutely everyone, knows how to use basic computer programs. They are not a luxury, this is vital knowledge for key moments, like artificial respiration or the Heimlich maneuver when someone is choking."

"Do you mean to suggest that my chances of surviving a fishbone stuck in my throat are better if I know how to use a computer?" Stojan Zec made no effort to mask his sarcasm. "Perhaps there is a special computer program that could help me succumb to death more readily, with less of the kicking and flailing?"

"Don't be silly," said Nemanja. "And besides, didn't you tell me once that the death of the body is nothing compared to the death of the soul? And that the loss of intellectual curiosity is a sign that from that moment on the person walks the world like an empty sack?"

Stojan Zec tried to protest, to say that he couldn't have said anything of the kind, but Nemanja had already slipped from the room in that amazing way available only to sixteen-year-olds. They'd look truculent, lazy when there was something that needed doing, indecisive when they had to get up in the morning, but there were times when they possessed the power of invisible propulsion through space, as if they were already living in a future where they would glide from place to place using only the power of the mind. There was no point in looking for him, Stojan Zec knew, because wherever he was, he was no longer in the same world as Stojan. Worst of all, the boy was right: his father had, indeed, said the words Nemanja quoted, maybe not precisely those words, but the message. He also knew when he'd said it: last year, on Nemanja's birthday, when Stojan had given him a large stamp album. As things later transpired, this was Stojan Zec's last attempt to make his son into a stamp collector. He had actually been trying for years, from the moment Nemanja started first grade, but the computer was already looming between stamps and the boy. What Stojan Zec liked best—the slow and patient removal of postage stamps from the moistened pieces of paper, drying them and then arranging them in albums—was precisely what most put off his son, and while Stojan Zec would talk about what he was doing, explaining how glue is best removed, what kind of paper is suited for the reliable absorption of moisture, Nemanje would be gazing longingly at the blind eye of the computer cyclops and imagining, no doubt, that he was furiously slaying the bizarre creatures that sprang from the corners of the screen or perhaps arranging twisted geometric shapes as they dropped faster and faster. Then Stojan Zec would explode with rage, the boy would burst into tears, his mother would rush into the room, and soon they would all be shouting at the same time and pounding and striding around the table, until the albums and catalogues were gathered up and stowed away on the shelf, where they waited for another day, which, Stojan Zec was more and more sure, would never come.

He did not understand why things were that way, though he guessed that the explanation had to do with the fact that the world had changed and that he hadn't caught on soon enough, or that somewhere in himself, even if he had noticed the change, he had done nothing to embrace it. To tell the truth, the world around him no longer much resembled his world. The countless screens, mobile phones, computerized libraries and galleries, virtual reality, all this contributed to his sense that he had stepped into a future he used to imagine while reading the science fiction novels of Clarke and Asimov as a boy. However he couldn't understand why this boy here had no interest in stamps, even in the world as it now was. Their worlds, after all, were still on the same planet, and the same sky still arched over them both, night followed upon day and then day followed upon night as it had for many thousands of millions of years. Why shouldn't his son feel the same thrill Stojan Zec had felt when he saw his very first triangular stamp? Why shouldn't a stamp from New Guinea or Costa Rica prompt him to imagine his life among the natives? Why shouldn't the faces of composers on stamps prompt him to listen to their music? Because the world, Stojan Zec had to admit, was not the same, regardless of the sky and stars, the east and the west, spring and fall. It was actually less clear than it had been before, but his son, he realized, would have to find that out for himself, when the time came.

Because of this he had decided the previous year, though he knew how Nemanja would react, that he would give the boy a stamp album for his birthday. He went over and handed him the present. Nemanja touched it, shook his head, and then unwrapped the wrapping paper. "I knew it," he said, set the album down and reached for the other gifts.

"Open it," said Stojan Zec.

Nemanja sighed unhappily, and then he slowly opened the album. On the first page there were stamps already neatly arranged. He didn't stop to see what country they came from, but he saw there were drawings or photographs on all of them of computers, keyboards, printed circuits, monitors, and computer mice. Some showed the faces of people he didn't recognize, but who clearly had something to do with the origins or development of computers. He closed the album and looked at his father. "Thanks," he said, "but this still doesn't mean I'll collect stamps."

"You don't have to," said Stojan Zec, "it is enough that you are interested in what the stamps depict. As long as there is curiosity, there is no cause for concern. The death of the spirit, believe me, is much worse than the death of the body."

Perhaps it wasn't right to be speaking of death, any death, during a birthday party, but it is always like that with children of that age— if there is a moment for a lesson, seize it, because one never knows whether there will be another. Nemanja, of course, never opened the album again, so it was probably every bit as dusty as the envelopes in which Stojan Zec stored the stamps he snipped off letters. He hoped that one day Nemanja and he would soak all those stamps in a dish full of warm water, and then slowly, their fingers bumping, they would rinse the glue off the backs, and then line them up on dry white paper and press them with heavy books. And after that, he decided, he would take Nemanja to the post office, and while the woman who worked behind the counter looked for new and beautiful stamps, Stojan Zec would hunch down, though he knew there was no longer any partition between them, and tell her, not without pride, "This is my son. He collects stamps."

I HAVE ALWAYS envied travelers who enjoy flying. The world is like a speckled pear for them around which they wing their way as fast as they can go. Maybe that is the way it should be. In this day and age, which despises slowness, planes are not a luxury but instead a way to assert one's place in the present and with which, moreover, one can steal a few hours from one's past or future, and that is a magic which is hard to resist.

I have been resisting it for years. It wouldn't bother me at all, indeed I would be overjoyed, if I could still travel by coach. The world no longer has the time, however, for a horse's trot, or even a gallop, and therefore, no matter how much I have fended off the charm of speed, I boldly step onto airplanes and obediently do the bidding of the stewardess. I buckle up my seat belt, check the life vest and the compartment from which the oxygen mask will drop, if needed, then I look down the florescent strip that will guide me, in the case of an emergency landing, to the nearest exit. Then I don my earphones, find the jazz channel, open a book and try to fall asleep as soon as possible.

That is what I did this time, too, at the beginning of the flight to North America. I was on my way back from Europe, returning from a meeting of writers from the former Yugoslavia, who, according to the concept put forth by the foundation that had organized the meeting, were to build a path to a new understanding, but instead it just brought the old differences to the fore. I don't know why I had been expecting something different. I was filled with bitterness, instead of with joy, and slowly but surely, as the plane climbed to its cruising altitude, the bitterness turned to a nausea that no pill could assuage.

There was nothing for it but to close my eyes during the steep ascent and then later, once the plane had reached its altitude, to submerge myself in other worlds. I had brought with me on the trip one of Isaac Bashevis Singer's books, a paperback in English, the novel *Enemies: A Love Story*. Someone might think, I thought, that my choice was tied in some way to the reason for the trip to Europe, that in this mingling of hatred and love, paradoxical at first, was hidden the key that could explain what the writers had not able to agree upon. The truth was different. When I fly I cannot read postmodernists: their fragments irritate me and the dislocated narrative exacerbates my fear of flying. Classic prose like Singer's calms me, draws me into its semblance of reality, and helps me forget where I really am.

Then I fell asleep. I woke just as the woman sitting on the seat next to mine leaned over to pick up the book that had slipped off my lap. A raspy man's voice was singing somewhere deep in my ears that this night would never end, though daylight was all around us as I could easily see through the little airplane window. The woman turned to me and held up the book. The yellowish liver spots on her face, neck and upper arms showed that she had long since become accustomed to age. I removed my earphones.

"Singer," she said as if I didn't know. "A marvelous writer. Do you know that story of his about how he saw Hitler in the middle of New York?"

"Yes," I said. My mouth was dry.

"I spent a night with him."

"Hitler?"

"No," she said, "I would never have allowed myself such a thing. I meant Singer."

I said nothing. What was there for me to say?

"I know what you're thinking," said the woman, handing me the book. "But it wasn't like that. I was teaching at a university in Wisconsin and Singer came to give a talk on Yiddish literature. I went up to him and said I had experienced something unusual, that I was certain I had seen Hitler once in Chicago. That caught his interest and he invited me up to his hotel room after the dinner he would have to attend with the head of the department. I went, and why wouldn't I? He greeted me still in his suit, he hadn't even taken off the tie, the only change was that he was wearing soft leather slippers. He said he couldn't bear the chafing of the shoes. He listened to me attentively, nodded his head, encouraged me to continue. He said that the world is full of illusions, but that we never know what is genuine. Nothing is merely good or evil, wise or stupid, happy or sad, there is always the possibility that one will turn into the other. He told me how he had swung from one extreme to another in his life and that he was never sure when he was awake and when he was dreaming. And what can I say? One word followed on another and there we were watching the sun come up. He was still smiling, but his was the smile of a tired man. 'Now I have to sleep,' he said, and fully dressed he lay down on the bed and immediately fell asleep. I sat for a while longer in an armchair and listened to him breathe deeper and deeper. The sky was all pink, a new day was dawning. I stood and went over to the bed. He was frowning in his sleep as if he didn't know what to do with the dreams. I leaned over and kissed him on the forehead. Then I saw his things laid out on the dresser by the bed. His wallet, fountain pen, notebook, a pocket watch. I reached over and took the watch to have a look at it, and then either Singer turned over in his sleep or a pigeon landed on the windowsill, I can't remember which, but the next moment there I was, outside the room, in the corridor, on the stairs. It was only when I'd left the hotel and was near the town square that I realized I was still holding it tightly."

She reached into her purse and pulled out an old-fashioned pocket watch and popped open the lid. I saw an engraved inscription: "To dearest Isaac from Vanda."

"Vanda who?" I asked.

"I don't know," answered the woman, "and I don't care to. A year later, in *The New Yorker*, or maybe *The Atlantic*, I saw the story about Hitler. He had changed a few things, moved it to New York, but there could be no doubt, this was the story I had told him that night. Since he had my story, I kept his watch. Fair enough, eh?"

The rattling of dishes drew our attention to the stewardesses who were pushing a cart down the aisle between the seats and serving lunch. After lunch, a voice announced over the loudspeakers, we would be watching an action movie and the latest news. The woman snapped shut the lid and put the watch away in her purse. I was afraid she'd stop talking. I asked her:

"Did you really see Hitler in Chicago?"

The woman looked at me and then turned to lower her tray. A sly smile played on her lips. Many years ago, I realized, that smile might have been enough for Singer to invite her to his hotel room.

"Everyone must see Hitler once in their life," she said. "No need to go to Chicago for that."

THE BASILICA IN LYON

1.

THE STORY begins in Lyon, but it might end anywhere. There are four men in the story, two policemen, five women, a couple of cameras, a bicycle (not visible), and an old soccer ball. The story has ten parts of differing lengths. The longest stretch of the story, covering more than one part, takes place in front of a basilica; the shortest part passes in almost total silence; all the parts are figments of the imagination. At one moment, even before it began, the story was out on the edge of town. It stood there for a while until rain began to fall. It brushed away the drops that were coursing down its face and stuck out its thumb. Two women were in the car that stopped. Both were chewing gum. "You can sit in the back," said the woman who wasn't driving, "or here between us, as you like." She shrugged and blew a bubble. The story thought it would be sad sitting alone in the back so it sat between the two women. The woman who was not driving slammed the door shut and the car pulled away. "Where were you headed?" asked the story. "Anywhere," answered the woman who was driving. Good, thought the story, I started in Lyon and I might end anywhere. She smiled first at one of the women, then at the other, then she closed her eyes and dropped off to sleep.

2.

She dreamed of ants crawling around on her, but when she opened her eyes she saw it was the fingers of the woman who wasn't driving. The woman had unbuttoned her blouse and was touching her skin with the tips of her fingers. The girl pushed the woman's hand away with disgust and buttoned up her blouse.

"What's wrong?" said the woman. "All I wanted was to see what your skin is like. You have nice skin," she continued, "but surely you knew that before."

The girl said nothing. She went on buttoning up her blouse and then she tucked it into her pants. Lucky thing I didn't wear a skirt, she thought. That morning she had spent nearly two hours deciding between a skirt and jeans, and though she'd been angry at herself at the time, now she was glad. She turned to check whether her backpack was still on the back seat: there it was, perhaps a little shoved to the side, but the padlock, as far as she could tell, hadn't been tampered with. The girl then looked out through the windshield and saw it wasn't cloudy outside, as she had thought it was when she woke up, but that instead it was getting dark. Headlights were lighting the road, but when the girl looked to the left and right, she couldn't see any lights. Who knows how far they had gotten from Lyon, she thought, and told herself that she mustn't ask them to stop. Then she heard herself say, "Stop, I want to get out."

The woman who wasn't driving began to whimper.

"For God's sake," blurted out the other woman, "will you shut up?"

The woman who was driving looked at the girl, "And you, what do you want?"

"I want to get out," said the girl.

"Here?" said the woman who was driving, "Are you certain?"

"Yes, I am," answered the girl. Actually, she had never been *so* uncertain.

The woman put her foot on the brake. "I won't be coming back for you," she said to the girl, "is that clear?"

"Yes," said the girl. She turned and reached for her backpack.

The woman who was driving touched her hand. "The backpack stays," she said.

The girl couldn't believe her ears. "What do you mean—it stays? All my things are in it."

"Exactly," said the woman.

Then the woman who wasn't driving started whimpering again. She whimpered louder than she had before, and with each intake of breath the whimpering got louder.

"OK," shouted the other woman, "OK, let her take her fucking backpack, who cares!"

The girl dragged the backpack over the back of the seat with effort. She waited for the woman who wasn't driving to get out of the car, then she got out after her. "Thanks," she said to her, and extended her hand. The woman who wasn't driving stared at her hand and whimpered even more loudly.

"Come on," shouted the woman sitting in the driver's seat, "get back in already!"

The car started up before the woman who wasn't driving had had a chance to sit back down. The girl watched the car move off into the distance, saw its lights get smaller and smaller, and then, when they vanished altogether, she turned in the opposite direction, put her backpack back on her back and set off with sure step, as if she knew where she was going.

3.

She woke up, huddled, on damp grass, in a ditch by the road. She didn't know how she had gotten there. She remembered the fear that had gripped her more and more as her steps rang in the dark. She'd have given anything, she thought, to be back there between those two women, a little touching never hurt, but it was too late to change. She could only walk and hope that a car would happen by, which she had begun to doubt, while meanwhile she had to get used to the sounds of the night which she heard on all sides. For a while she was convinced that someone was walking along the other side of the road, then she heard the snapping of branches right by her and she stopped, frantic with fear. The branches continued snapping for a while longer, but she convinced herself that the sound was moving away and she kept on walking. An assortment of night birds could be heard, but she couldn't tell them apart. They were all owls to her, though for the creature which flew by her face she quite rightly decided that it was not a bird, but a bat. If only she could be a bat, she moaned, and find her way in the dark. Her exhaustion draped over her like a ragged dress and she probably stumbled over something at that point, sat down beside the road and fell asleep. She stood up and looked around. It was early yet, a mist slid over the fields, the leaves on the trees shuddered, the road was damp. She didn't dare think what her hair was like, and her make-up was probably smeared, she must have looked a fright. Then she heard the sound of a motor and saw a car. She raised both her arms high, felt her blouse pulling out of her jeans, and wondered whether this was some sort of sign, but by then the car had stopped and out of it peered a middle-aged man, graying hair, gray moustache.

"We are out early this morning, aren't we," said the man.

"It's a long story," said the girl.

"Will it take all the way to Lyon?" asked the man. "Or at least to where the city begins?"

"No problem," said the girl, "it can take even longer than that. My stories are always under absolute control."

"Fine," said the man and only then did he look her up and down. He told her to put her backpack in the back, he waited for her to sit beside him and fasten her seat belt, and then he drove off. He drove courteously, perhaps even slower than necessary, because at first the fog was extremely dense. Later, when it thinned and then lifted, he drove faster, but still cautiously, avoiding every risky traffic situation, so the girl felt her eyes closing. If I fell asleep, she thought, would he unbutton my blouse? She imagined his palm on her stomach and it didn't bother her, but she didn't want to test him or herself.

"How are you now," asked the man, "have we woken up at last? A night spent in the woods sure can throw off the rhythms of body and mind."

The girl rubbed her eyes. The facades of houses were moving past them and she realized that she had, indeed, dropped off to sleep. She looked down at her blouse, but not a single button was undone. She checked the buckle on her belt, though she quickly thought she was overdoing it a bit. She yawned once, twice, and asked where they were.

"In Lyon," said the man, "where else would we be?" He looked over at the girl. "You wanted to go to Lyon, I hope I didn't get that wrong?"

"Oh, no," answered the girl, "I mean, oh, yes, sure I wanted to come to Lyon, you weren't mistaken."

The man smiled and said, "Where should I leave you?"

"Leave me?" asked the girl. "Why?"

"Well, presumably you are going somewhere," said the man, "and I wanted to take you there."

The girl caught sight of a little cluster of white tents. Colorful flags were hanging on many of them. Some of the tents were open and there were people gathered out in front. "Here," said the girl, "this is where I was going."

The man didn't say anything. He slowed down, then he stopped, he waited for the girl to get out and then he handed her the backpack. He took out his wallet, found a business card and gave it to the girl. "I work in a museum," he said, "if you are done before lunch with what you came to do, come and find me, perhaps we could have lunch together." He watched the girl studying the business card and smiled. "The museum isn't far from here," he said, "everyone will be able to show you the way."

4.

The girl waved as he pulled away, then she turned toward the tents. She had no idea what was going on here. The tents gleamed in the morning sun, somewhere there was wistful music playing, pebbles rolled around her sneakers, it occurred to her that she didn't even know what she looked like and ran through her hair with her fingers, then she passed by the security people and wandered from tent to tent. A different country was in each tent and the girl quickly picked something up to read explaining that this was a consular exhibition, that all the countries were displaying their economic and cultural achievements, including folk art, music and dance. The girl put down the brochure and continued her amble among the tents. She tried to discern the pattern of which tents were open and which tents were closed, she tried seeing the pattern as related to national traits, but soon she saw there was no pattern. The Croatian and Serbian tents, for instance, were open, while the Bulgarian and Greek tents were closed, though they all belonged, if she was not mistaken, to the same Balkan region. She went into the Serbian tent and studied reproductions of medieval frescoes. A young man who was sitting at one of the tables coughed softly, which was a sign that he was available to answer her questions, if, of course, she had any.

"I have no questions," said the girl.

She spoke over her shoulder, in a half-turn, and the young man hadn't heard her properly. He got up and went over to her. "If I understood you correctly," said the young man, "you had some questions?"

The girl turned and saw that the young man had the same eyes as one of the angels. "No," she answered, "I said I have no questions."

The young man shrugged and smiled. "Sorry," he said, "it's the music."

And sure enough, one of the tents across the way had music blaring. The girl didn't know what sort of music. She thought of China, Korea, Indonesia, and later, when the music ended, she no longer thought of anything. She turned and saw that the boy had sat down again by the table. She went over to him, quickly, as if she didn't plan to stop, and he suddenly looked at her with his angel eyes. "I do have one question after all," said the girl. "Where is this museum?" She took out the business card and handed it to the young man.

"Oh," said the young man, "it isn't far, you can walk there from here." He turned to look around him. "I should have a map of Lyon here somewhere," he said, "I'll show you."

"If it is so near by," asked the girl, "couldn't you take me there yourself?"

The young man stopped shuffling through the things on the table. He stared at his hands for a minute, as if he were expecting an answer from them, then he drew a mobile phone from his pocket and dialed someone's number. While he spoke in a language she didn't understand, the girl leafed through books about the monasteries in Serbia. The young man finished the conversation and stretched. "As soon as she comes," he said as if the girl knew who he meant, "we can go. You'll see, it really is close," he continued, "but if you aren't sure, no point risking it. People get lost in Lyon easily and disappear without a trace."

5.

The young man went back as soon as they got to the museum. He said he had to hurry, that the secretary of the consulate could stand in for him for only half an hour, that the consuls of Japan, Canada and Australia had made appointments to visit the Serbian tent, and that the girl had only to walk through the courtyard and she'd find herself at the museum entrance. The girl wanted to ask something else but he was already hurrying away and disappeared among the passersby. She took out the business card and then, while the ticket seller at the cash register called the man the girl wanted to see, she sat on a chair in the corner to wait.

The man who appeared ten minutes later, went over to the ticket seller at the cash register and then, when the ticket seller gestured at the girl with her chin, came over to her and asked how he might help her, was not the man who had driven her to Lyon that morning. The girl took out the business card again and gave it to the man.

"Yes," said the man, "that's me."

"No," said the girl, "that's not you."

The room was silent.

"I must know who I am," said the man. His voice suddenly grew inflexible and hard.

"Then how did I," asked the girl, "get your business card?"

"I'd like to know that myself," said the man. He turned to the ticket seller and shouted: "She doesn't know where she got the business card!" The ticket seller nodded in sympathy.

"I got it from a man who drove me to Lyon this morning," answered the girl.

"You only arrived in Lyon this morning?" exclaimed the man, surprised. "Why that's incredible!" He turned to the ticket seller again and shouted: "Can you believe it, she only arrived in Lyon this morning!" The ticket seller nodded again in sympathy.

"What is so strange," asked the girl, "about me getting to Lyon only this morning?"

"You got here this morning," said the man, "yet you're talking as if you were born here. That is incredible. Would you allow us to test you?"

"No," said the girl, "I've got to go."

"She has to go," shouted the man to the ticket seller. The ticket seller only blinked and picked up the phone.

The girl suddenly realized where all this might be headed. She stood up abruptly, shoved the man away with all her might, and as he tumbled across the armchair she ran outside. In the yard full of greenery and shadows there was no one; the only thing on a bench by the entrance was an old soccer ball. The girl didn't stop; she kept going, out into the street, she turned right, in the opposite direction from where the young man from the Serbian consulate had gone, then she turned into the first street to the left, then again to the right, then again to the left, until she felt she was lost. Then she came out into a little square and thought she'd like to sit down.

6.

The girl sat at a table in a restaurant in the little square. The chimes of church clocks reached her from time to time, but she never counted from the first ring, so she had no idea what time it was. Most recently she counted out three chimes, and when she'd counted before that, she counted five. She raised a hand to call the waiter, but when she asked him, he also had no watch.

7.

Then night fell. Abruptly—though the day, the girl thought, still hadn't reached its end—but perhaps that was how night fell in Lyon, as if waiting in ambush. From the place where she sat and was having her third espresso, she couldn't see across the square. The darkness was dense and tangible, so she kept brushing it off her face and picking it out of her hair. She wanted to pay, but she could no longer see the waiter (just as he, probably, couldn't see her), so she got up and looked for the door to the restaurant. She found a door, which she hadn't seen before, opened it and stepped into a room full of people.

They were standing in groups of three and four, deep in conversation and paying no attention to each other. Someone did notice when she came in, stopped talking and stared at her, and soon all the little groups were standing there, silent, staring at the girl, and the only thing audible was the pat of her footsteps which proceeded, though she had no notion where she was. Since I got to Lyon, thought the girl, I know less and less and soon I won't know anything at all. There are cities like that, she thought, in which you seem to disappear, as if melting into the houses and streets, unlike those cities in which you grow and multiply and are always becoming someone else. She couldn't remember any such city, though there was a wisp of memory hovering in her of a small town in which she saw herself as if she were slipping around a corner, but now she was in Lyon, or at least she hoped she was in Lyon, and she had to forget everything else. By now she had made her way back to a narrow door on which the word "Exit" was written and when she reached for the doorknob, the clamor came back to the room. No one looked at her anymore. Nor did she look at them. She opened the door, went out, shut it behind her and leaned against the wall. Her heart was pounding so loudly that it reverberated off of something. The girl thought: Finally I have arrived. On the ground, between her feet, she noticed a crumpled envelope and now she reached for it. On the envelope were the words: "For You—Open Immediately". "How did they know," said the girl, "that I am here?" She looked to the left, she looked to the right, but there was no one nearby who could answer her. There was a slip of paper in the envelope on which was the message: "I am waiting for you by the basilica."

8.

"Excuse me," the girl asked a policeman the next morning, "where is the basilica?"

The policeman raised his eyebrows, clearly surprised, and then gestured skyward with his head.

The girl laughed. "I didn't mean the basilica in heaven," she said.

"I meant is there a basilica here in town, in Lyon?"

The policeman kept on gesturing with his head and making grimaces, until he realized he was getting nowhere. "Not in the heaven, my dear," he said, "right here on the hilltop, up on the hill!"

The girl looked up and, sure enough, right above her on the hill she could see the basilica. It seemed as if all she needed to do was jump up to reach it, but later, when she panted as she went up the steps and steep paths, she cursed the basilica and the letter and whoever wrote the letter and herself and especially Lyon which, so harmonious and beautiful, was stretching out before her more and more, gradually filling the whole horizon.

So what now, thought the girl when she had finally reached the basilica around which large and small groups of tourists were walking, how will I recognize the person who wrote to me?

"Sorry," said a youngish man, "would you be willing to take a picture of me in front of the basilica? Everything is all set," he said and handed her the camera. "All you have to do press the button."

The girl took the camera, studied it on all sides, and asked, "This button here?"

"No," said the youngish man, "the other one."

The girl placed her finger on the button, waited for the youngish man to take his pose, and then she pointed the camera in his direction, but when she looked at the little screen, she saw only the basilica. The youngish man stood on the steps and grinned, but no matter how much the girl tried, his figure did not appear in the image.

"Are you done," asked the youngish man, "may I step away?"

"Sure," said the girl. If she handed him the camera quickly, she thought, and then turned and went, maybe he wouldn't notice anything, or when he did notice it would be too late. She didn't actually know why she should be feeling guilty about this, but she had already had it with Lyon and everything that had been happening to her there. What a story she could put together of all of this!

The youngish man was speedier than the girl had imagined, and, without breaking the movement with which he took the camera, he brought it to his eyes and looked for the picture the girl had taken. "Brilliant," he said, "you take photographs like a professional, we came out beautifully!"

The girl came slowly over to him. She looked at the little screen and saw what she had seen before: steps and no one standing on them. Yes, she thought, high time for me to leave Lyon.

"Would you like me to take a picture of you standing in the same place," asked the youngish man, "or somewhere else?"

"No," said the girl, "I want to go home."

"All of us want to go home," replied the youngish man. "It won't take but a minute or two anyway, not even that."

The girl didn't like it when other people pleaded with her. "Fine," she said and went over to the steps. She didn't know where the youngish man had been standing exactly, so she decided on the sixth step.

"Great," said the youngish man, "exactly where I was standing."

"Just a minute," said the girl and raised her hand to her face. "That's what I was just thinking."

"Coincidence," said the youngish man. He kept holding the camera pointed at the girl.

"There is no such thing as coincidence," replied the girl, "there is just someone's readiness to believe in coincidences."

The boy shrugged and said that he did believe in them.

"So I thought," said the girl and sighed. If he believed in coincidences, then he was not the man who had left her the message. But, she stopped, why am I saying "man"? Couldn't it have been a woman? And while the flash went off on the youngish man's camera, the girl began to look at women out on the terrace in front of the basilica.

9.

"I see you are looking for me," said a small woman who resembled a mouse. She came slowly up to the girl, step by step. Until she stopped on the second step. Then she moved up to the third.

The girl wasn't fond of anyone standing so close to her on the steps, least of all a person whom she didn't like, but she also knew that if she herself went up a step or two, the small woman would keep coming closer. That's how it is with mice, thought the girl, you can't stop them. And then she said, "I'm not looking for you, you are looking for me."

The small woman stood on the fourth step. She said, "Who is looking for whom is not what matters, believe me." She breathed with effort, as if she had only just climbed up the hill to the basilica. "What matters is who will find whom."

"Was it necessary," asked the girl, "to climb up here to the sky beneath the clouds?"

"We are far from the clouds," said the small woman, "and farther yet from the sky."

The small woman raised her right foot, lowering it onto the edge of the fifth step, and the girl felt herself break out in a sweat. I must pay no attention to this, she said to herself, though she didn't stop even for a second staring at the woman's foot. "So what now?" she asked, "Is this all?"

The small woman said nothing for a moment, then she suddenly moved up to the fifth step, lifted her face to the girl, and said, "I have a bicycle."

The flash that went off just then was not on the camera of the youngish man who, the girl concluded, had vanished without a trace. It was on a camera held by a fat woman who, obviously, had been listening to their conversation. "In Lyon," said the fat woman, "everyone has a bicycle."

"Who asked you?" snorted the small woman. "You'd do better getting out of my sight this minute before I scratch your eyes out!"

"Who are you to talk to me like that?" said the fat woman. "You really gave me a start, that's for sure. Look at her, would you?" she turned to the girl. "If I were to sit on her there would be nothing left."

"With an ass like that," said the small woman, "you are lucky you can get up at all."

"Midget freak," screamed the fat woman.

"Lady elephant," shot back the small woman.

"Ladies, ladies, don't go on like that," a voice could be heard behind the girl's back, "what will our guest think of us?"

The girl turned and saw a policeman. He was the same policeman who had shown her where the basilica was. Even if he wasn't, thought the girl, he looked enough like him. There was no difference anyway between one policeman and the next.

"Oh," said the policeman, "you're wrong there. True," he said, "every uniform makes the people who wear it look alike. After all that is the whole purpose of the uniform, but that doesn't mean that each of us isn't different, distinct, full of all sorts of emotion, love, joy and sorrow." His voice began to quaver so he stopped talking for a moment. "There," he said in the end, "this morning my rabbit died."

"Why, that's a terrible shame," said the girl.

"Poor bunny," said the fat woman.

"So sorry," said the small woman.

"What will you do now?" asked the girl. "Will you buy a new bunny rabbit?"

"Oh, no," said the policeman and brushed away a tear, "that would be too soon. First I need to grieve the loss, so that the wound in my heart heals, then I plan to attend a brief course on mastering pain so that I can face reality, and only then, after all that, I might decide to buy a nightingale."

"Ah," said the small woman, "I always wanted a nightingale."

"I'm not sure," said the fat woman, "that's a good idea."

The girl said nothing. Everything happening in front of the basilica stirred in her the feeling that she ought to be careful. Simply put, she could not believe that all those people just happened to find themselves near her, and she couldn't understand why such a large group of people would be working to draw her into some sort of game, a game, furthermore, about which she understood nothing. And on top of all this, the policeman had read her thoughts a moment before, after which, in fact, she was doing all she could to think nothing, to be an empty mirror, until the moment arose for her to slip away and go somewhere else. That is the way it is with stories: they might begin in Lyon and end anywhere, leaving traces as they go, just as a dog trots around and marks its territory. One of these days, who knows when, the story would come back this way and pick up the ready fragments just as a person picks fruit when it's ripe.

And when she thought of that, the girl raised her hand, signaling to the policeman and the women to stop talking.

"You needn't talk any more," said the girl, "because there is no rabbit nor was there ever one."

The women were shocked, the policeman tried to object, but the girl, with a grin, cautioned them, wagging her finger.

"There's no cause for anger," said the girl, "because life, though it looks as if it belongs only to us, is a story being told by someone else. That is why we met here in front of the basilica, because in each of us is a story in which we play a role, but all those stories are different and each of us has to find our own. The story in which we find ourselves is the wrong one and we got here because the storyteller was careless, but if we leave now, and if we hurry, perhaps we'll still find the one we are supposed to be in. A story, after all, which begins in Lyon needn't necessarily end there. The real basilicas are inside, not outside, of us."

10.

Nice job, said the girl to herself once the policeman and women had gone. She didn't know what she'd do, but if she was patient enough, something would occur to her. Good, she thought, I'll wait, what matters is that the story is winding down. Maybe the end doesn't look like an ordinary ending, but then again Lyon is no ordinary city. She had understood this as she climbed up the stairs and sought the path leading up to the basilica. Her legs shook with the effort, sweat coursed down her face, her throat was dry as sandpaper, and she didn't like Lyon at all, but when she'd reached the basilica and looked down at the city from the surrounding terrace, she believed she would stay here forever, curled up under a tree or on a bench, in a darkness she didn't fear. A story can't feel fear, she thought, it can only quake at the thought that it might be interrupted or chased downhill, but at least as far as that was concerned, after the climb, this was no longer a cause for fear. When a path leads downhill, everything goes much more easily.

IN ALL HONESTY, Ruben was at a loss to explain what was happening to him. He told his friends and family a story about feeling tired and drained, while in himself he saw a different sort of picture: somebody, who knows who, some huge and powerful being, was squeezing him the way the last squirts of toothpaste are squeezed from a toothpaste tube. The crush of those huge fingers, the blunt thumb and the slightly angular index finger, produced so much pain at times in Ruben that, lying in bed or mid-stride, he could barely hold back his screams. His life, he realized one morning, had become, over time, the anticipation of pain, as if nothing else mattered and as if the pain had become a measure for all that shaped his life. His visits to doctors produced no tangible results, all his test results were fine, or, at the very worst, on the border, but never beyond it, over onto the other side.

"From a physiological perspective," a doctor told him, "your health may not be the best it has ever been, but close to it, at least as far as your body is concerned," he added. "So you have nothing to worry about."

"What should I do, then," asked Ruben, "which direction should I take?"

The doctor touched his forehead in passing, as if embarrassed, then he touched his temple. "It may all be in the head," he said finally.

"In the head," said Ruben, surprised, "what do you mean?"

"Everything is in the head," answered the doctor, "though many fail to understand that."

Judging by the tone of his voice, suddenly tender as if he were speaking to a child, Ruben realized the doctor meant him. He could, of course, have been offended—after all, it was as if the doctor were telling him he was crazy—but he didn't allow himself that. He smiled, shook the doctor's hand and went off to pay for the visit. While he was waiting for his receipt, the doctor appeared again and handed him a sheet of paper with the address and phone number of a woman, a colleague of his, whom, he said, he trusted completely.

Ruben looked at the sheet of paper only when he'd gotten home. The name Violeta Puhalo was written out in large letters. There was a phone number next to her name, but no address. Ruben crumpled it up and tossed it into the wastepaper basket which stood by his desk. Ten minutes later he pulled it out and smoothed it, then he stared for a long time at the name and number. He picked up the phone, set it back in the cradle, then picked it up again, and, without allowing himself to change his mind, started dialing the number.

The voice was different from everything he'd expected and that unpredictability made him immediately accept her suggestion that he come for an introductory session. "As soon," said the voice, "as possible." She had already spoken with her colleague, the voice went on to say, and he, her colleague, felt they should waste no time. The voice suggested they see each other on Monday.

"I hate Mondays," answered Ruben.

"So much the better," said the voice, "that way we'll tear down a barrier right from day one and open the pathway to each other."

Ruben pictured himself for a moment as a lone demonstrator, surrounded by a fence with various slogans. Would everything really get better once the fences and the obstacles were gone? He asked what time would be good, he wrote the address and phone number down, though the number was the same number he already had, but he stopped writing when she said her name.

The voice asked him if he had gotten everything down. "If you need," the voice said patiently, "I will repeat all of it again."

"Violeta," said Ruben, "is not such a common name."

The voice hesitated for a moment, and then added, in order not to lose rhythm, "What do you mean by that?"

"Exactly what I said," answered Ruben. "There aren't many women these days with that for a name."

"Does that mean," asked the voice, "that you already know a Violeta?"

Ruben could feel the voice grow surer. "I have known three Violetas," he said finally.

The voice barely noticeably lost rhythm. "Will you," said the voice, "tell me about them?"

"I already am," answered Ruben.

The voice stopped. Ruben pressed the receiver against his ear, but he heard nothing. Then he had the impression that he could hear someone breathing. "Hello," he said, "Violeta?"

"See you Monday," said the voice and rang off.

*

Monday began with a gloomy morning, sunless, as if everything had a uniform, colorless tone and seemed brittle and fragile. A real morning for hatred, thought Ruben as he stood by the window and scratched himself. He was scheduled to meet with Violeta at eleven, which meant he had plenty of time to take a shower, shave and get dressed, and even change his clothes if he didn't like what he had selected. He thought, also, that it was amusing to be thinking of his meeting with her as if he were going out for a date with a woman, and he assumed this was some sort of defense mechanism piping up inside him being as he was going off to see a psychiatrist. Ruben, actually, wasn't sure whether Violeta was a psychologist or a psychiatrist, but he sensed that this didn't make much difference, at least in his case. Like most people, he felt mistrust of these professions, because he believed that they could, as if they had some special kind of x-ray vision or scanner, see everything that was in his soul, and even things that no longer were in his soul. And not only what had been in his soul, but even what was to come, because if they didn't have the power to see future events, how would they have the knowledge to heal?

The view of the door leading to Violeta's office was of no help, because her name was the only thing on the door. He touched his finger to her bell, then removed it, checked what he was wearing and ran his fingers over his clothes, checked that there wasn't a button wrongly buttoned, fixed the knot on his tie and chided himself for not wearing a hat. He looked over his shoes, then polished them on his trouser legs. Now he could ring the doorbell and it responded with a cheery melodic ditty that Ruben recognized but couldn't pin down. So as soon as the door started opening, he asked, "What is that melody your doorbell plays?"

The woman who came to the door had red hair and long finger-nails done in a clear, colorless fingernail polish. Without changing her broad grin, she repeated Ruben's question and, as if she didn't know what he meant, she rang the doorbell once more. The cheery melody filled the hallway. "I don't know actually," said the woman, "but I could look at the instructions, they probably say."

Ruben suddenly wondered whether the woman there in front of him was Violeta, with whom he had arranged to meet, but he didn't know how to ask.

As if she heard his unasked question, the redheaded woman put forward her hand and said, "I am Violeta."

"Oh," said Ruben. He touched her hand and immediately re-leased it.

"I know," smiled Vioelta, "you didn't expect me to look like this. The red hair confuses everyone." She moved a little to the side and invited him to come in. "There is no reason," she said, "for us to waste time." She looked at her wrist watch. "Another patient will be coming at noon."

"I am not a patient," said Ruben, but still he went into the ante-room. The door softly closed behind him, and for a moment, after the unusually bright lights in the building corridor, he found himself in a protective gloom. Violeta walked by him and the sleeve of her blouse brushed against the fabric of Ruben's jacket. She opened the door that led into her office and stepped directly in, without waiting for Ruben. He moved slowly, much more slowly than he meant to, and when he finally entered the office and shut the door, Violeta was already seated at the desk. Ruben looked around and with regret saw that the fabled couch was missing; instead, in the corner there were two armchairs, facing each other.

"Of course you're not a patient," said Violeta, "we will talk about that later." She gestured toward the armchairs. "Would you like us to sit there?" she asked, "More comfortable for conversation?" She flipped opened a file that was on the table and peered into it. "Your doctor," she said, and touched her forehead and temple in passing, "thinks that the real solution to your complaints should not be sought in your body."

"I know," said Ruben.

"Do you agree with him?"

"I am not a doctor," answered Ruben.

Violeta was persistent. "You needn't be a doctor," she said, "to have an opinion about your health."

Ruben said nothing.

Violeta repeated the invitation for them to sit in the armchairs, and then, as if to give him an example, she sat down first. Ruben hesitated a moment longer, then he joined her. He believed that when he sat down he would sink into the armchair, but it was surprisingly firm, and, he had to admit, quite comfortable.

"And now," said Violeta and crossed her legs, "you promised you'd tell me about the Violetas you have known."

"I fucked the first one standing up," said Ruben. He saw how Violeta's eyes widened though he saw no fear in them or a call for caution. To be perfectly frank, he had surprised himself by his own words. He had never expressed himself so vulgarly before, especially in front of a person he didn't know, but now it was too late. He couldn't take back the words he had said, and anything further he could say would only worsen the already bad impression. He breathed in deeply and counted to ten before he breathed out.

"And," spoke up Violeta, "how was it?"

"Clumsy," said Ruben and laughed. His laughter was hollow and artificial, he could hear it himself, he didn't need a psychologist or a psychiatrist for that.

"I understand," said Violeta, "not the most comfortable pose, especially if there is a big difference in height."

"A stool," said Ruben.

"Sorry?"

"You need a stool," Ruben explained patiently.

"In other words," said Violeta, "you always need to have a stool handy."

"Yes," agreed Ruben, "a folding stool."

"And the third one," asked Violeta, "what happened with her?"

"You've skipped the second," said Ruben.

"I did not," answered Violeta, "I'm saving her for later."

Ruben studied her face closely. He couldn't rid himself of the impression that she was toying with him, that she knew everything about him and was only pretending to ask him questions. How, for instance, had she known that that the second Violeta in his life should be left for the end, since she, that second Violeta, had so made her mark on his heart that he sometimes wondered how had he survived at all? Of course, he cautioned himself, when one is talking with a psychiatrist or a psychologist, whatever she was, one doesn't speak of marks on the heart but of marks on the consciousness, about the structure of mechanisms of remembering and forgetting, of guilt and ridding oneself of guilt, about the unconscious and the subconscious. He could have gone on with the list, but he sensed this would change nothing. "The third," he said, finally, "was not important."

"Nothing is unimportant," countered Violeta. "Every part of our lives, at least at the initial level, has the same value. Nothing is purely good or bad in and of itself, meaningful or meaningless, instead we make it what it is."

Ruben couldn't take his eyes off her. He asked, "Are you sure that's so?"

Violeta lost her rhythm again. She waited a little longer than necessary, just a little, but enough so that Ruben concluded he was winning. And, of course, as soon as he thought this, he chided himself for seeing things that way. He hadn't come here to compete, he had come to learn something about himself, but what?

"I am sure," Violeta said finally.

Ruben no longer knew what her answer referred to, because he was still caught up in the dilemma of his competitive spirit. "The third Violeta," he spoke up suddenly, "has almost completely gone from my memory, I am no longer even sure her name was Violeta."

"There's no reason for you to be angry," said Violeta, "and if you aren't enjoying this conversation, we can stop."

Ruben felt her overtaking him and taking the lead, but he could do nothing about it. This reminded him of dreams in which he watched helplessly while something horrible happened to him, but he was never able to warn himself. He'd open his mouth, widen his eyes, flail his arms, everything was futile: no voice came out of his throat, no warning rang through the air, he could only moan while he watched himself falling from a cliff or sinking into a fresh crack in the earth's crust. He never saw himself dead, not even from afar, and he believed that his consciousness was protecting him that way from the unpleasant sight of mangled corpses. He looked at Violeta and asked, "Why is it that we never see ourselves dead in our dreams?"

Violeta returned his gaze and he could see that her eyes were more alive, interested, her whole face, in fact, shone, and she sat up in her chair, straightened her shoulders, patted her hair. "Whatever gave you that idea," she answered, "when that is not even so? Why," she went on, "just last night I dreamt that I was lying dead on the floor in the front room, while a man's voice could be heard from the other room, saying my name."

"From which other room," asked Ruben, "here or the kitchen?"

"Here," said Violeta.

"Why not the kitchen?"

"In the dream I knew that there was nobody in the kitchen."

"And now?"

"What now?"

"Do you now know," asked Ruben, "that there is nobody in the kitchen?"

A trace of insecurity flashed in Violeta's eyes for the first time. She wasn't afraid, that was also evident, but she no longer had enough self-confidence. Soon, Ruben thought, she will start looking longingly at the phone, and at that moment Violeta started glancing over at her mobile phone, back on her desk. If she were to get up now and go over to it, she would be admitting she was afraid, and she, Ruben sensed, would never do that. He tried to judge how much farther he was from the phone than she and he concluded that he probably could grab it before she did, especially if he lunged suddenly. Instead, he was surprised by Violeta's belated answer.

"I am sure," she said, her voice trembling a little, "that there is no one in the kitchen, but I am not sure why you mentioned your own dead body in the context of a conversation about the Violetas. Did something tragic happen to the second Violeta?"

"If something had happened to her," answered Ruben, "why would I dream my own dead body?"

"That is a switch that typically happens in dreams," said Violeta, "especially in a case when someone won't admit their guilt, and then the subconscious attributes the death to itself, or rather, it says: It would be better if I were dead, and that she, or he, or anybody, were alive."

"A dangerous thing the subconscious," smiled Ruben. He did not miss noticing that Violeta, pretending that she was getting more comfortable in the armchair, had moved an inch or so closer to the desk.

"The subconscious doesn't lie," said Violeta.

"I didn't say it lies," replied Ruben.

Silence settled. Ruben stared unblinking at Violeta. He saw her touch her forehead, but then, instead of touching her temple, she dropped her finger to her nose. Again she crossed her legs and leaned even more toward the desk. Ruben knew that she knew that she mustn't stop talking, but nothing was coming to mind to talk about, or, more likely, nothing that came to mind gave her any sense of security. Then she mustered her courage. This was evident from the way she quickly licked her lips and brushed the hair away from her face.

"You killed her," said Violeta, "isn't that so?"

Ruben finally took his eyes off her and looked down at his hands.

"No," Violeta nearly screamed.

"What?"

"You strangled her, didn't you?"

"Never," said Ruben and stopped talking.

"What?"

"I would never do that," Ruben said through clenched teeth.

"I can't say why," said Violeta, "but I do not believe you."

Now she was poised to stand. Her legs were no longer crossed and she was leaning with one hand on the edge of the seat. Always that hope, thought Ruben, that fate can be changed, that it is possible to win a race which you are slated to lose. Her wrist, almost white from the pressure, was so slender he could have snapped it like a twig. He heard her bone snap as clear as a bell, at once both sharp and dull. But she heard it, too, and not just once, but twice. Her body abruptly relaxed, the shadows cleared from her face, her hand rose from the seat edge.

"What was that," asked Ruben, "did something happen?"

"The cleaning lady," answered Violeta nearly triumphant, "the cleaning lady came in."

And sure enough, there were sounds of a door opening and closing, of someone walking, hesitating, moving some things, and then the sounds disappeared and it was quiet again.

"How do you know," said Ruben, "that was her?"

"I know," said Violeta, rising suddenly, grabbing her mobile phone and, without a break in her movement, striding to the door of the doctor's office, she opened it, stepped out and quickly closed it behind her. He soon heard her speaking to someone, then the person replied, then there was a brief silence, then someone's steps slowly, cautiously, neared the door of the office, a key jangled as it slid into the lock and then turned twice. The steps moved away, followed by hushed whispering, and then there was nothing else to be heard.

Ruben did not move the entire time. He knew Violeta was now dialing the police, he could imagine what she would say, how she would urge them to hurry, because, who knows, she was telling them, what he is prepared to do, she could see by his behavior that he was crazy, that he was obsessed, and after all he had all but confessed to killing a woman whose name was the same as hers, perhaps he is obsessed by the name, no, the person is no relation of hers, she has no idea who the person is, but hurry please, and we, the cleaning lady and I, no, her name is not Violeta, she just happened in and has nothing to do with the man, in any case we will go out and wait for you by the front entrance.

Ruben got up and went to the window. He opened it wide, leaned out and looked down. The office was on the third floor, and if he found no better solution, he would be able to jump to the roof of the kiosk that was in front of the building and reached up to the second floor. He turned and surveyed the office, then he went to the desk and looked into the file that had his name written on it.

The file was empty. He looked under it, peered under the desk, but found nothing. He looked around and saw his own face in a small, framed mirror. He didn't know how he had gotten there. Maybe he should take the mirror down from the wall, remove it from its frame and free himself that way? He turned toward the wall, heard the front door slam, he flinched and hurried over to the window. He stood with his left foot on the sash, then his right. He imagined Violeta's startled expression when she saw him at the entrance to the building and he smiled. His muscles tightened, especially his stomach muscles, but then he realized he'd never dare to jump. He tried again, but his thighs wobbled, his hands went limp, his knees went all soft and shaky, he had to sit. Above him, he noticed when he looked up, stretched a perfectly empty sky. He had never seen anything so simple and so beautiful. He swung his legs back and forth, whistled a tune from his boyhood days, and while the sound of the police siren grew louder, he tipped forward until he felt himself losing his balance and that the weight of his head was drawing him down. He closed his eyes and tipped his head forward a little more, ever so little, but far enough.

"ELI RAISED his leg and caught sight of Earth. It was smaller than he'd thought it would be, no bigger than a marble, though shinier and more vibrant. 'Terra,' he whispered, 'terra nostra,' and then he checked around him cautiously: sometimes a whisper, he knew, carried further than the loudest shout. No one, however, looked as if they'd heard: not the man sitting across from him reading a paperback, nor the woman at the adjacent table peering at the screen of her laptop, nor the man at the bar who couldn't have heard him anyway over the hissing of the espresso machine. His gaze flitted over the things which, forming a sort of irregular pattern, stood on the table: two ashtrays, a dish with a moist tea bag, a little spoon amid sugar granules, a cigarette lighter, a crumpled napkin, a kernel of corn, and two worn coins. Of course, he thought, everyone will want to know how the kernel got here, though it matters the least of all these things, in fact, it means nothing, because soon a little bird will come and eat it.

"And sure enough, only a moment later a sparrow landed, looked left-right, approached the kernel of corn, and downed it. Then it gave the ashtray a peck, wagged its beak and flew off.

"If there was a microphone concealed in the ashtray, thought Eli, the tap of its beak must have reverberated like a cathedral bell in the ears of the people listening in. He imagined their heads jerking and them hastily yanking off the earphones, and he chuckled.

"The man sitting across from him suddenly arched his eyebrows. Laughter, Eli knew, was frowned upon and he tried to be serious, but the more he tried, the more gasping his laughter became, until several policemen burst into the restaurant, surrounded Eli as he was laughing, and raised their truncheons in unison..."

Here I stopped and said nothing until the woman coughed and asked: "So what happened next?"

"I don't know," I said and shrugged. "The story stopped here and I can't seem to take it any further. As if it were crouching in a hole in the wall, deep enough so I can't reach it, yet at the same time wide enough that you get a sense of the story's hem."

"A story has a hem?" asked the woman, surprised. "That's the first I've heard of it. Are you sure?"

"Not just a hem," I said with a grin. "A story can have a lining, patches, pleats and shoulder straps."

"It's going to turn out in the end," said the woman, "that stories are stitched in tailors' shops."

"Precisely!" I exclaimed and several people turned to us. "A writer is a tailor, and a story is stitched like a shirt. And just as a shirt is always assembled of more or less the same parts, so the story is always, essentially, the same. The details, however, are what make it current, up-to-date, in step with the latest fashion craze. The basic structure of the shirt never changes, it's only a few of the parts, like the collar and cuffs, the close-fitting or loose-cut waist, the shape of the pockets and—"

"I get it," said the woman, "you needn't enumerate every detail. And besides, I know how to sew. I may not write stories, but I understand what you're saying."

I bent my head so she wouldn't see the admiration flash across my face. Ever since she and I had first met my conviction had been steadily growing that for me she was ideal. But, did I really know her? I wasn't sure, just as I wasn't sure whether the torrent hadn't simply dumped her on my doorstep or whether we had met on an imaginary outcropping, safe for now from sinking and collapse. In any case, I didn't know her name, where she was from, or how old she was, all of which showed that we had not been formally introduced, yet perhaps there was something we could accomplish together, for instance: shoot an elephant or rhinoceros on land, and then, as we waded into the ocean, there would be waiting for us a blue whale, the largest mammal in the world. Before that, of course, the apartment needed a tidy-up and every thing had to be put away where it belonged. I wasn't sure where to stow the tea strainer so I dropped it at random into the third drawer from the top. The tea was somewhere else, up in a cabinet, which I found confusing, this business of separating things that belong together. The fact that the pot for heating the water for tea was in the pantry along with all the other metal pots and pans pushed my confusion to the limit.

I scowled and the woman immediately asked if I had a headache.

"No," I said, "my head isn't aching, it's that I'm feeling uncomfortable about being in a strange apartment."

"Nonsense," said the woman, "this apartment isn't strange, it is my place, and we," she said and smiled, "are hardly strangers."

I looked at her smile and didn't know what to do. I raised my leg, but down below saw nothing, not even a worm. I looked at the woman and she patiently waited out my stare. Then she said, "Of course, it all depends on whether the things you said before you fell asleep on the bench by the promenade last night are true..."

"Before I fell asleep?" I repeated, filled with admiration at her kindness. "It would be more precise to say: before I lost consciousness from the vast quantity of alcohol I imbibed." I remembered that at one point we left the hotel to take a walk, but from that moment on, all I can see in my mind's eye is darkness, darkness, and more darkness. I had no idea, for instance, how she'd gotten me to her hotel room and dressed me in a large white T-shirt with the words "Don't ask! Just do it!" I woke up next to her in bed, and she was naked, tangled up in the sheets and with a pillow between her legs. I leaned over and brushed the hair off her forehead. Without hair her forehead was like a boy's, so I moved three or four locks back to where they had been, thinking as I did that we should all have our pictures taken so that a database could be put together which would be handy for everyone.

Afterwards I forgot about the database and it came back to mind only much later, as so often happens, when I wasn't thinking about anything. I suddenly realized I was staring at a large box, carefully packed with books, and I thought of the database and almost burst into tears when a voice said, "Everyone will be in there: father, mother, two small children, their toys, your books and shoes, shirts and sweaters, LPs and photographs, and all of it in peerless order, arranged from A to Z, so that it is always extremely simple to find things."

All of this had parched my tongue—rolling in my mouth like a log; it turned my speech into mumbles, a series of dead words, into the sticky story-telling of someone with no teeth.

"I don't understand any of it," said the woman when we'd reached the far end of the promenade, "and it all sounds like a story slapped together in a great rush."

I had no choice, I had to go back and tell it from the beginning. "While I was walking through the park," I said, "I caught sight of a woman whom I immediately felt had been made for me, that we were fated to meet here in the park, and that we'd never part again. I know," I said, "that these are old-fashioned ideas, hopelessly romantic, but the feeling in me was so powerful that I couldn't breathe. Without hesitating a moment I went over to the woman, drew her away from her company and told her of the feelings welling up inside me and which, as her face grew larger and larger and more precise before my eyes, showed a growing aggressive streak. 'Oh, replied the woman,'" I said, and looked at her, and she went on, "'Oh,' she said, 'this is the most thrilling day of my life and of course I want to play my role to the end, I would never miss such an opportunity.'"

"I can tell you that a great boulder rolled off my heart at that moment. It rolled off and laid between us until I kicked it aside. When I looked up again at the woman, her eyelids fluttered as if she were waking, though clearly she was the most rested and lively of us all. I say this as if there were a lot of us there, but we were only three: the woman, me, and the boy who never leaves my side. The three of us were so tired we were propped up against one another like books on a shelf, which meant that at any minute, booklike, we might tip over. I have been woken many a night by books toppling on overstuffed shelves! And every time I thought I would change the shelves and buy new ones, or, perhaps, spruce up the ones I have. I had all the tools handy, all I needed to do was start." The woman coughed gently, warning me not to go on branching the story in so many directions. "Tell about what came later," she said, "when you grabbed my hand and I said to you: 'Who are you to be holding me by the hand?'"

"Who am I," I repeated, "to be holding you by the hand?"

"Yes," said the woman. That she was anxious was evident, that she feared even her own shadow, that she was prepared to shrink so far that no one would ever find her, but I doubted they would allow such a thing. I sent the boy to arrange for three places by the wood stove and that I'd said we'd sleep there, and that they should ready three cots for us. I could, of course, have gone up to the second floor, and gone into my childhood room, but I was not in any shape to sustain the flood of nostalgia that would have had me sobbing in bed. 'Nothing worse than tears in a bed that creaks,' I said out loud, once we were already under the covers by the wood stove, 'because with every sob, every gasping breath, every tear that courses down the face and drips into the ears, the bed creaks more, so that all is left is for you to wish you are gone, that everything come to an end'."

"Oh, my boy, my poor boy," whispered the woman and reached toward my face, but instead of caressing me, she poked her finger in my eye and I howled like a kicked dog.

From all sides came words of protest and open threats, and I whispered into the woman's ear that it would be better for us to get out and take a little walk, at least until the tempest in the room had subsided.

"Yes, of course," said the woman hastily, "oh, of course. Just let me put on my slip and I'll be right with you."

"She wears a slip," I repeated, elated, while I stood in the chilly vestibule, "she wears a slip!" I had always been partial to slips and she couldn't have said anything sweeter to my ears. No, there was no longer any doubt in my mind that she was made for me, ideal no matter how one looked at her. And I didn't hesitate to tell her so as soon as I caught sight of her, especially as her slip was showing exactly as much as needed, two centimeters, maybe an inch, something like that. I took her by the hands and told her what I meant to tell her, that she was made for me and that with her I could even venture into my childhood room. "I want to tell you everything," I said, "every moment of my life, where I was when John F. Kennedy was assassinated, when Tito died, when Slobodan Milošević was arrested, and when man landed on the Moon."

The woman said she wasn't sure all of that interested her very much. She was already carrying so much information, she remarked that her head sometimes dropped from the sheer weight of it all. "There is nothing so weighty," she concluded, "as information. After all," she said and raised an index finger, "how many times has it happened that people have died while sitting in front of their television sets, crushed under the weight of the news and the sheer quantity of information coming at them from every corner of human existence. We surely don't want anything like that to happen to us, now do we?"

"Oh, no," I said.

She looked into my eyes, and said, "But you can tell me a story whenever you like."

"Really?" I came to life. "Whenever I like? Even now?"

"Absolutely," she said, "Even now. Especially now."

"Any story?"

"Any story at all," she said. A moment later she added, "Except ones with rude language."

And so I began to tell the story of Eli and his seeing Earth when he'd raised his leg. Earth was called Terra. Everything else had no name, as if coming from a new world as yet undiscovered, though that world, judging by Terra, knew precisely where it was. The woman listened attentively and from time to time she'd purse her lips, which stirred the narrator and influenced the rhythm of the story-telling. Once he even stopped talking altogether, but no one from the audience said a word; post-modernism had taught them they could expect almost anything from new prose and poetry, including interference at a number of levels of content and time. Reality dipped into the imagination and out of it like a butter knife or a honey spoon that would be used for nothing else.

The woman listened to me with her mouth open. I saw her tongue, I saw her teeth, I saw the dark that led to her throat. Had she been able to swallow me she certainly would not have hesitated. That is why I had to go on with the story, this is how I defended my life, this is how I stayed alive. But at one point, when I stopped talking for a moment to take a breath, she spoke up before I did and said, "The man from the beginning of your story, what was he afraid of? Why was he whispering?"

It took me time to remember what she meant. Then I smiled and said I didn't know. In all of it, I went on, what mattered to me was the sentence about how he raised his leg and caught sight of our

Earth. I was entranced by the image and for days I had been wondering where he had been, what he was doing, and how he'd managed to catch sight of Earth. I thought the cosmos was a playground for giants of vast dimensions who tossed planets back and forth the way we toss balls...

"You are lying," said the woman, "you're lying something awful."

I looked at her. No one had accused me of lying for so long that I didn't know how to respond, what to say. And besides, she was right: the beginning of the story wasn't mine; it was actually the slightly altered beginning of a story from an old anthology of tales of fantasy and science fiction. I didn't know the author's name, but I knew what his narrator feared: while in exile on a distant planet (which was described as if it were an outer space version of a Soviet gulag), where mentioning the name of our planet was forbidden, he was afraid he'd be heard by an interloper, and for this violation he would be sentenced to an additional five years in the frozen gulag.

"This is the truth," I said to the woman, "you've got to believe me!"

"So that means," the woman said thoughtfully, "that the beginning of the story isn't yours?"

"Exactly," I said, "it isn't mine."

"Well, if the beginning isn't yours," she said firmly, "then the end needn't be yours either."

"Exactly," I repeated. It was so cold in the gulag that I was ready to acquiesce to anything.

The woman smoothed a wrinkle on her uniform and straightened her cap. She stood in front of me, legs akimbo. "The end is mine then," she said. "Is it not?"

"So it is," I said once more, but without looking up. What happened next was up to the woman anyway: a kick, the snap of a whip, a gun shot, but nothing like that happened. "Look at me," said the woman and when I finally did I saw she was naked. "The next time you go to Terra," she said, "promise you'll take me with you." "Of course," I said. The wind suddenly gusted and the woman looked as if she were not walking but flying. I waited for her to reach the gateway to the camp and then, pulling my cap down over my ears, I hurried after her.

MUNICH GHOSTS

1.

JOZEF HAD come to Munich by chance. He was on board a plane that was slated to take him to Frankfurt, but the captain addressed the passengers at one point and said he had had to change the flight plan and they would soon be landing in Munich instead of Frankfurt. He added something else by way of explanation, first in English and then in German, but there was already such a commotion on the plane that almost nothing could be heard, and so Jozef never learned whether this was in response to a threat, mechanical trouble, or weather conditions. "As long as it isn't terrorists," he said to an anxious elderly woman sitting next to him. "Everything else is easier to take."

The old woman did not answer. She rolled her eyes, clutched at her chest, and gasped raggedly, so much so that Jozef finally summoned a stewardess.

The stewardess glanced briefly at the anxious old woman and said there was nothing she could do to help her just then. "We are busy responding to the panic and dismay," she said. She squeezed Jozef 's shoulder, bent down and whispered in his ear, "Give your mother a little hug, that will do the trick." Then she straightened up, winked, and left.

Jozef thought he should call after her to say this wasn't his mother, but he gave up. He turned to the old woman and saw she had nodded off. A thin stream of saliva drooled from her mouth while her eyelids fluttered like butterfly wings. The captain made another announcement, saying they were descending into Munich and Jozef quickly collected his belongings and returned them to his bag. The old woman no longer woke, even when the plane wheeled to a stop.

"Where is your mother?" asked the stewardess standing by the exit from the plane. "Is she feeling better now?"

"Much better," Jozef answered, and then added, "She fell asleep and I didn't want to wake her, so later you can take her where you like."

The stewardess's eyes widened, but before she had a chance to say a word, Jozef walked by her and joined the other travelers who were protesting noisily upon stepping into the terminal building.

The representative of the airline first tried to calm them, then he stopped talking and waited for them to quiet down. "Unforeseen difficulties," he said then, "contributed to our decision to land the plane in Munich. The company will do all it can to see to it that most of the travelers continue on their travels today, though we already know that some will have to spend the night in Munich. The travelers whose name I call," said the airline representative, "will be given a voucher for a hotel near the airport, as well as coupons for lunch and dinner, all at the expense of the airline." He thanked the travelers for their understanding and began reading the list of travelers for whom accommodation had been arranged at the hotel. Among them was Jozef.

2.

The hotel was not only right by the airport, it was also, as the clerk explained with patience to Jozef at the reception desk, near a train and bus station that would bring him to the center of Munich. Jozef collected a heap of brochures, took with him a map on which the clerk at the reception desk had marked a number of tourist attractions, and went off to the hotel restaurant to have lunch. During the meal he worked out a plan for how he would spend the rest of the day, asked the clerk a few more questions at the reception desk, and hurried off to catch the bus.

So it was that at about four o'clock in the afternoon Jozef was in the very heart of Munich—Marienplatz. Then he realized he had forgotten one thing: it was Saturday and there was such a crush of people on the square that he was barely able to take more than a few steps in any direction. Everyone was staring upward, as if under a spell, at the tower of the New City Hall where there was a glockenspiel, though it was next scheduled to chime almost an hour from then. Elbowed from all sides, Jozef kept checking the contents of his pockets, and then, squashed into a corner of the square, he decided to step into a bookstore by whose window he happened to be standing.

He spent almost an hour in there, less focused on the books that he could only have leafed through anyway, and more on coffee in the restaurant on the top floor. As he was leaving the store the bells of the glockenspiel began chiming their cheery melody. In fact the melody wasn't so cheery, and as soon as he had moved a little ways off Jozef could no longer remember it, but even if it wasn't cheery, it certainly wasn't glum. Indeed, packed with tourists as it was, Munich did not seem to be a dreary city. I should go to a beer hall, Jozef thought and shivered with a delicious thrill at the thought of a cold beer, but first he had to go to somewhere else which was not, judging by the map, far off.

3.

In fact it was close. First Jozef came to a big department store and went in, compelled by the thought of buying something, but quickly gave up because of the crowds of customers. Then he left, turned right and walked down into St. Jakob's Square. Here, somewhere on the square, should be his destination: the new building of the Jewish Museum, recently opened—he had read about it in the press—as a sign of a new burst of vitality in the Jewish community. Jozef wasn't interested in the museum collections on display, because he knew what price had been paid for the earlier loss of vitality and could no longer face exhibits showing it. He simply wanted to see the new building, thereby keeping, as his friends would say, well informed. And furthermore, even if he had wanted to tour the exhibits in the museum he wouldn't be able to because it was Saturday, Shabbat, when the museum was probably going to be closed.

The museum was open after all. At first, as he neared the cube-shaped building, he thought that the people he discerned through the darkened glass were only a reflection of pedestrians on the square, but when he turned he saw the square was nearly empty. In fact, except for a young man in a leather jacket and Jozef himself, no one else was out just then in its expansive spaces. Jozef continued circling around the building, studying the perimeters and faces of the museum cube with curiosity, and trying at the same time to see better what was going on inside. He noticed that the man in the leather jacket was following him, staying several steps behind. He turned to see. The man looked down hastily and began brushing crumbs from the sleeve of his jacket with great attention. Who knows how long he would have kept this up had Jozef not reached the door to the museum, pushed it open, and stepped inside.

His attention was immediately drawn to books for sale, piled on tables, and dedicated to an assortment of Jewish subjects. The man in the leather jacket did not follow him in, but another young man, this one in a dark suit, who was standing near the entrance to the exhibition halls, did not take his eyes off Jozef. Jozef shrugged and kept on perusing the books. He finally settled on two, both about traces of the Nazis in Munich, paid for them and headed toward a small restaurant on the other side. The man in the dark suit continued staring fixedly at him and Jozef barely resisted winking back. He ordered coffee, sat, and dipped into the dark world of the books about the Nazis and the Holocaust.

He must have dozed off, not realizing how tired he was, and he was woken by a bang so loud that he almost fell from his chair. For a moment he had no idea what was going on and he was about to seek shelter if need be. Then he realized the loud bang was made by the book dropping from his hand; the book had led him to dream he was at a beer hall where a group of Nazis were roaring song after song. Though Jozef did what he could to make himself invisible, they soon spotted him and the loud bang came from a table tipping over and being shoved aside, and he was behind it. He tried to lurch to his feet but they rushed him on all sides, pulling his hair, snatching his eyeglasses, tearing his shirt, pummeling him in the chest and stomach and for first time Jozef seriously feared for his life. He shut his eyes for a moment and when he opened them again there he was at the museum restaurant and everyone was looking over at him.

"You are the third person today who dozed off here," a man told him who was sitting at the next table, "and all of them were sitting

DAVID ALBAHARI

right where you are now; they must be up to some experiment." Jozef followed the man's suspicious gaze that raised ceilingward, then wandered up and down around it and finally settled on an upper corner. He saw nothing, no equipment over which such an experiment might be run. And besides, he thought, for experiments like that they would need to have the permission of the examinee, and no one had asked him anything. He turned and saw that the man in the dark suit no longer had his eye on Jozef; now he was watching two young women who were commenting quite loudly about the books on the tables by the entrance. At one moment they moved apart, which prompted the man in the dark suit to say something into a small microphone on his lapel, and a moment later the man in the leather jacket entered the restaurant. One of the women, meanwhile, had walked into the restaurant and taken a seat at the nearest available table, while the other went off to the exhibition hall. The man in the dark suit went after her straight away; the man in the leather jacket continued to stand near the restaurant. His gaze flew over the other guests and, when his eyes met Jozef's, Jozef nodded to him as if he were an old acquaintance.

The man in the leather jacket did not respond to Jozef's greeting. Who knows, thought Jozef, maybe he doesn't really know me. Had Jozef become someone else after the dream? He looked over at the man at the next table and asked him, "What is going on here?"

"Here?" repeated the man, confused. "What do you mean? They organize shows, lectures, readings at the museum..."

"No, I meant something else," said Jozef, but when the man asked him what, Jozef only shrugged. He wasn't able to explain. Something was off, something essential had changed after his dream, as if he had passed from one reality to another where he did not belong, which could mean, he warned himself, that in fact he no longer existed. He looked through the darkened glass and saw that St. Jakob Square was teeming with people. Where a moment ago there had been no one in the square but the man in the leather jacket – now in the museum —the square was so crowded you couldn't have inserted a pin among them, yet people kept thronging in, waving banners, and marching songs thumped, the voices of speakers rang out, and there was no sign this would be wrapping up any time soon.

/124

Then from somewhere rang out a shot, if it really was a shot. It was more like the loud bang of a cork popping out a bottle of champagne, though Jozef was sure this had been a pistol shot. He didn't know how he knew since he had never fired a gun in his life, but he was soon proved right, because the man in the dark suit appeared at the museum entrance holding his hands high over his head. The woman was behind him with a pistol and suddenly everyone began to shout and scream, drop to the floor, and crawl under tables. Only Jozef didn't move. He sat motionless, certain that nothing would happen to him, and saw the man in the leather jacket take out a pistol in a seamlessly practiced move and hit the young woman in the forehead with a precisely aimed shot. The other woman, her friend, leaped from her chair and tore off her jacket so that everyone could see the explosives and wire wrapped around her body, but before she had a chance to do anything the man in the leather jacket was faster and a little circle appeared on her forehead too. The woman began to fall, grabbed for the chair, kneeled and said, "Fuck, it's not working, no blood."

The first woman, lying on the floor, lifted her head and said, "I have enough blood for you and me both, though I can't figure out why shit like this always happens to you."

The man in the dark suit dropped his arm, rubbed his left shoulder, and said, "It doesn't happen just to her, look, you fucked up too. You didn't put the swastika on your sleeve."

"Impossible," answered the girl, and then looked down at her sleeves and laughed. "I guess not," she said. She took out tape with a swastika on it and tossed it at the man in the dark suit. "If you had had to study last night for a fucking exam," she said, "you would have left your shithead behind, too."

"Stop the swearing," said the man sitting at the table next to Jozef's. "If you make a mess of something, swearing doesn't make it better."

"We thought," said the woman with the explosives, "that the swearing would make us tougher and more dangerous."

"Swearing only makes you stupid," said the man and then he turned to Jozef. "What do you think?"

Jozef hesitated with the answer. "I am a little confused," he said in the end, "I don't know what to say."

"So," asked the girl with the pistol, "you believed us?"

"Almost," said Jozef, "the only thing I wasn't sure of was how it tied in with all the people on the square."

"What people?" the girl was surprised. "There is nobody on the square!"

Jozef looked through the darkened glass and sure enough, the square was empty.

"It wouldn't be a bad idea to move a part of the performance out into the square," said the man at the next table, "but the municipal authorities wouldn't allow it. They'd think it too risky for security."

Jozef said nothing. He didn't dare look out there again, though he knew that sooner or later he would have to get up and leave the museum building. Regardless of whether the scene on the square was part of a dream about the past or a dream about the future, he wanted nothing to do with it. So he sat in the museum restaurant until they announced closing time.

4.

After all that Jozef didn't feel like going to a beer hall any more. He ambled for a while longer through the old part of town, frequently consulting his map, and followed a tangled web of little streets and passageways which he hadn't expected to find in Munich. He turned from time to time, thinking the man in the leather jacket was following him, but never spotted him. At one point, when Weinstrasse came out at Marienplatz again he veered suddenly into a restaurant and went up to the second floor. While he sat sipping a cappuccino nobody who came in showed any interest in him. Meanwhile, through the window he could see the sky darkening, night advancing, and by the time Jozef was out in the square again the city looked different. Noisy groups of young men and women were clustered at the entrances to the restaurants and clubs, cars made their way slowly through the narrow streets, different languages and musical rhythms mingled, and Jozef decided it was time to go back to the hotel.

His return was monotonous, Jozef thought as he stepped off the bus, and had been like conquering a forgotten silence. This didn't last long, however, because a plane rumbled overhead as it climbed toward the dark sky. Rain could fall from a sky like that, thought Jozef and picked up his pace. He hurried in vain. Not a drop fell on him, but he trotted into the foyer of the hotel panting and perspiring.

He went over to the reception desk to ask whether any information had been left regarding the next leg of his trip the next day, as the airline representative had promised, but the woman at the desk couldn't hide a smile when she heard his name. "Good timing," she said, "I was about to write you a message. First of all, we have moved you to another room."

"Another room?" repeated Jozef. "Why?"

"That first was a single," answered the woman, "but now you have a double."

"I don't understand," said Jozef. "Why would I need a double?"

The woman gave him a pitying look, as if she had suddenly realized she was speaking to a person of limited mental capacity, and said, "Your mother is using the other bed."

"My mother!" shouted Jozef. "What are you talking about?"

"The hotel is full," said the woman calmly, "so we couldn't give her a separate room. And besides the airline representative assured us you wouldn't mind."

"Look," Jozef went on shouting. "My mother died seventeen years ago and I have no clue what you're talking about." And then, as he was speaking he remembered the old woman who had been sitting next to him on the plane. He didn't know how this misunderstanding could have happened but the old woman clearly didn't know or wasn't able to explain her situation and then the stewardess, who had already decided he was the woman's son, had concluded she should be accommodated with him. He remembered the old woman's befuddled gaze and he had to admit that his mother had had a similar look in her eyes in the last months of her life. Someone bumping her in passing would send her into a tizzy and no words could reassure her. "Fine," said Jozef to the woman at the desk, "fine, just give me the key."

The woman looked at him with suspicion. "Are you sure," she asked as she handed him the key, "that your mother won't be a nuisance?"

Jozef turned to walk toward the elevator, stopped, and said, "How could one's mother be a nuisance?"

5.

The Jozef's bedside lamp was on, so his fears that he might trip in the dark were unfounded. The old woman was sleeping on her side, with her back to Jozef. She breathed deeply and quietly, and every once in a while she made a soft, throaty sound. Jozef didn't dare lie down on the bed, for fear the woman might wake up and be shocked by the sight of a strange man. So he chose to spend the night in the armchair where he was quickly overcome by sleep no matter how hard he tried to stay awake.

He woke up in the middle of the night, his neck stiff. The light was still on, but the bed on which the old woman had been sleeping was made up and empty. The bathroom was also empty, and even looked as if it not been used. His suitcase and several items of clothing were in the room, but nowhere could he see the old woman's things. Jozef got up went over to the old woman's bed, knelt, and peered under it. Then he peered under the other bed, opened the cupboard in the hallway, pushed aside the plastic shower curtain around the bathtub. He finally had to admit that the old woman was gone.

He told this to the man at the reception desk. "Old woman?" replied the receptionist and stared. "What old woman?"

Jozef stopped for a moment, and then said, "My mother."

The receptionist made plain his surprise. "You have lost your mother?" he said. "Do you know when you last saw her?"

"Here," said Jozef, "at the hotel. When I came into the room last night, she was sleeping; when I woke up she was gone."

The receptionist consulted the computer screen and said that, as far as he could tell, no one but Jozef had been staying in his room. Perhaps Jozef had imagined the whole thing, he added. Many people saw ghosts in Munich, because where there was a surfeit of historical traces, ghosts prospered. The gentleman should go back to bed, the receptionist said, and if the old woman appeared again, he should pay her no mind.

Jozef stood for a while longer in the hotel foyer, uncertain, then he returned to the room. He went over to the perfectly made-up bed on which the old woman had been lying earlier and stripped the bedding. He inspected the sheets and bedspread closely, then shook the pillow out of the pillowcase, lifted the mattress and pushed the whole bed away from the wall. Nothing.

He sat in the armchair and through the window he stared at the ever-lightening sky. He knew his life had changed irrevocably and that, no matter what he did, he would never be as he had been before. He waited patiently for the phone to ring. He picked up the receiver, heard what the airline representative had to say, and replied, "That's fine, thanks, but I will not be continuing with my trip. I will be staying in Munich."

LANA DESPISED Zurich. "All that residue of history," she said, "it's so awful! Like when you're out in a dense forest walking on layers of leaves and first you think how nice the sound of the rustling is underfoot, but when you lean over and breathe in the smell, it's all just rot and stench."

Stefan did not agree. Zurich for him, as he often said, was one of those cities in which the modern European spirit had been formed, a touchstone. "Just think of who has lived in Zurich," he said to Lana, "and you'll immediately see its greatness. If it were a stagnant swamp, as you say, they never would have come here."

"Yes," Lana replied begrudgingly, "Lenin and Tito did like it here."

"Tito was never in Zurich," protested Stefan, "not before or after World War II."

Lana made no effort to hide her anger. "How do you know?" she asked. "Was it Svetlana who told you?" She pulled away from Stefan and turned her back to him. Actually, what she was pining for was a cigarette—she always felt like smoking after making love—but two months had passed since she'd given up smoking, it would be stupid to start again, even if it turned out that Stefan really had been with Svetlana.

Stefan said nothing. He couldn't remember when it was he'd last seen Svetlana, but they had spoken for a while about Tito at the time. Svetlana was from Belgrade and had come to Zurich four years before. She had only planned a brief visit to her friend Milanka, a painter who had been living in Switzerland since the outbreak of the war in the former Yugoslavia, but Svetlana had managed to get the necessary papers and the visit stretched on. Stefan had met Svetlana the previous year at an opening of Milanka's latest show that he had gone to because his best friend, Max, who was working for a volunteer organization, was fascinated by people from the Balkans, particularly people from Serbia and Bulgaria. Max had known Milanka's former husband, Georgij, from Sofia. In a moment of distress

Georgij killed himself. After that regrettable incident Max kept up with Milanka so they all turned up at the opening of the show at the Incontro Gallery on Lutherstrasse.

Stefan was fascinated by Svetlana as soon as he set eyes on her and Lana quickly sensed it. During the opening she deliberately stood between them several times, but they went right on talking as if no one was there. Stefan, of course, denied it all later when they got home, though he wouldn't discuss it. He knew this was about ownership and that no protestations to the contrary would diminish Lana's fear of losing something she felt was hers. Stefan could tell her that her fear was not grounded, because what he felt for Svetlana had nothing whatsoever to do with ownership. Svetlana, he thought when he saw her, could be his friend, which he did not try to explain to Lana, since he knew she wouldn't believe him.

This sounded every bit as incredible, however, to Svetlana. "You want us to be friends?" she said, surprised. "Are you sure?"

Stefan nodded.

"Why that's wonderful," said Svetlana, she leaned over and pecked him on the cheek. "I have never had a man as a friend and I've always thought that would be nice. My heart is pounding like crazy at the very idea!" She grabbed Stefan's hand and tucked it in under her left breast. "Can you feel it?"

Stefan said he could and gently withdrew his hand. Friendships survive thanks to constant temptations, he said to himself, and this was clearly the first.

When they got together a third time, Svetlana began talking about Tito. She had been seven years old when Tito died. She heard the news of his death at school and while they stood there stiffly, listening to the sirens, tears coursed down her cheeks. She didn't stop crying, she said, for three days. Three days and three nights, she added, so her mother had had to change her wet pillowcase in the middle of the night. When she stopped crying, everything was different. With his death, she said, something was lost to her forever, and to bring it back she had to renew Tito within her. She bought a large poster of one of his wartime photographs and put it up on the door to her room so that his gaze, no matter where she was and what she was doing, was always on her. When she made love for the first time some ten years later with a high-school boyfriend she stared at Tito's eyes over the boy's shoulder. And while the boy did what he could so that everything would be right, Svetlana imagined she was giving herself to Tito and felt an indescribable pleasure wash through her body.

"So that is how I became Tito's girlfriend," she smiled at Stefan, "and that lasted for several years. All that time I brought boys to my room and enjoyed pleasure thanks to him. And then, with no warning, the magic stopped. Tito still caressed me with his gaze, but regardless of what my boyfriends did I stayed completely cold. I didn't know what was going on. I tried putting up other posters—Che Guevara, Marx, Mao—but none of them worked."

"Maybe you should have put up a poster," said Stefan, "of someone who was alive."

"I thought of that," said Svetlana, "but the result was the same, until one day I came across a photograph of Tito in a white suit, cigar in hand. I felt as if I'd been struck by lightning. Then I realized that a photograph has a shelf life and needs to be changed from time to time. Afterwards I found it was quite enough to keep a picture of him on my bedside table."

"And no one asks you why his picture is there?"

"Men don't ask much," said Svetlana, "when they are in bed."

"So what do you do when you travel?" asked Stefan. "Take a poster with you?"

Svetlana laughed. "I have a better solution," she said. She slipped her hand into her bosom and pulled out a heart-shaped medallion hanging on a gold chain and opened it. On the left side, very small, was the photograph Svetlana had mentioned: on the right there was a picture of just his face, laughing and jowled.

"And that does the trick?"

"Works like a charm."

Stefan didn't know what else to ask. Friendship, he thought, also has its limits. Svetlana, however, clearly needed no prompting. She went on talking about her obsession with Tito, how she read everything about him and dug around in the archives to resolve the secrets related to his origins and identity. She had traveled over most of

Europe to do so, she said, following his movements as a prominent international communist. When Stefan asked whether she had come up with something for Zurich, that is when Svetlana replied that Tito had never been to Zurich, not before or after World War II. The same sentence was what Stefan had repeated for Lana while she, with her back turned, wondered whether she would ever stop being obsessed by the thought of a lit cigarette and the desire to inhale the fragrance of the tobacco.

That was Friday night. Though she usually spent the whole weekend with Stefan, Lana suddenly decided to go back to her place on Saturday. She hadn't brought with her some of her things, she explained, and she didn't feel like coming back to his place and then, on Sunday, doing the same thing again. The next three days, however, she didn't call or pick up when he called, though they usually spoke several times a day. She only got back in touch on Wednesday, late in the afternoon, just as Stefan was getting ready to go over to her place. And, without giving him a chance to say a word, she quickly said, "Tito was, too, in Zurich..."

Stefan didn't follow at first what Lana was saying. When she reminded him, he burst out laughing. "I cannot believe it," he said, "here I've been beside myself with worry these last three days, and meanwhile you were getting back at Svetlana."

"I met with her, too," said Lana. "It's all taken care of."

"What is taken care of?" asked Stefan, "I hope you two didn't fight."

"Not at all," answered Lana, "we made up."

"I didn't know you'd quarreled," said Stefan.

"We could have," explained Lana, "but when she told me about her relationship with Tito, I saw there was no call for a quarrel. There is no room for anyone else in her life. Once I'd seen that, everything else was easy, though I had come well prepared for the other, more complicated version."

"I do not understand what you are talking about," said Stefan. "First I wanted to prove she is not always right, but that was something I meant to show you, not her. Then I went all over the place and found out that Tito had been in Zurich after all but his time here was so secret that few people know of it. Svetlana hadn't known either. I asked her. Later she completely changed. She opened up and then I learned all about Tito and her."

"But who told you," Stefan asked angrily, "that Tito was in Zurich?"

Lana signed. "Long story," she said and took a deep breath. It turned out that, not knowing where to turn, she'd done the best possible thing. She remembered a friend of her parents once long before telling her that his father had played a part in forming the Swiss Party of Labor near the end of the war. It occurred to her that he might have an easier time of finding out whether Tito had ever been to Zurich, so she called and told him what interested her. As if he had been waiting for someone to ask that very question, he told her that Tito had been in Zurich in 1940, probably at the behest of Moscow, in an attempt to stop the sudden plummet in membership following a ban on the activities of the Communist Party of Switzerland. He even showed her a photograph in which several people were seated around a café table and then he lowered his index finger to a man whose face was in the shadows. "This one is Tito," he said, "or at least it is someone who resembled him." Tito, he explained to Lana, always had a few doubles, so no one ever knew which one was the genuine Tito. There were people who believed that the Tito who ruled Yugoslavia was one of the doubles, said the man, and that the real Tito died in the war. Whatever the case, two days later Tito disappeared from Zurich, and the Swiss communists spent the war years underground until 1944 when the Party of Labour was formed. A year later, in December 1945, during the Third Congress, his father did not hide how disgruntled he was because, he said, they were not following the guidelines Tito had left as his legacy to them. His father hadn't said what sort of guidelines these were, and maybe that didn't matter, said the man, because he knew his father was more upset about Karl Hofmaier being chosen as secretary general of the party; Hofmaier was replaced several months later for his involvement in a financial scandal. His father, said the man, though seriously ill, did not hide his joy at that, and his last words were, "Thank you, Tito." Then he died.

"I told Svetlana all of this," said Lana, "at a restaurant. When I finished, she took three snapshots of Tito from her wallet and asked which one was like the person whose face I saw when I was with my father's friend. I took up the pictures, one by one, and the longer I looked at them, the more I understood Svetlana's fascination."

"Don't tell me," laughed Stefan, "that you have a poster of Tito now on the door of your bedroom."

"It was supposed to be a surprise," said Lana.

"You're joking," said Stefan.

"Come over, you'll see," replied Lana and hung up.

Sure enough, when Stefan came, Tito's poster was on Lana's bedroom door. She had even moved her bed and placed it so that she had a view of the poster, which had resulted in shifting other pieces of furniture. Are these signs of impending madness? wondered Stefan. Never, of course, would he dare say so aloud; and besides, what did he know of madness anyway? Once more he looked around the room, then he heard a soft patting sound. He turned and saw Lana perched on the bed; she was patting the bedding next to her thigh, inviting him to sit down beside her. Stefan came over slowly, sat and opened his mouth to say something, but Lana didn't give him a chance to say a word. She embraced him, covered his lips with hers and drew him down onto the bed. When Stefan opened his eyes a little later, his gaze met Tito's and whenever he tried, no matter where he looked, no matter how he turned, Stefan could see nothing else.

III

HOLDING HANDS

WE GAVE A party Thursday. There were seven married couples invited, a few divorced women and men, and four of my wife's students.
My wife teaches physics and chemistry to recent immigrants who
want further training or a change of vocation in order to fit into the
system of the country they have chosen as their new home. We told
everyone to come around 8, and by 8:30 there was such a ruckus in
the house that our cat didn't dare poke its nose out of the closet it
had crawled into when the first guests knocked at the door. The last
to come, a Japanese couple, arrived at nine. They bowed forever at
the door and apologized for arriving late, but in the end I did manage to steer them into the house. I also managed to figure out what
they'd like to drink—she wanted tomato juice and he asked for a
beer—and after I had introduced them around to the people standing near us, I went off to find clean glasses. I opened the kitchen
door, and there, in the middle of the room, stood my wife and a
dark-skinned man, and they were holding hands.

"Ah," said my wife, "you got here just at the right moment. This
is Ahmed."

They kept holding hands and, as far as I could see, they had no
intention of letting go.

"Ahmed is my student," said my wife.

Ahmed said nothing.

"Haruki and Hiroko have arrived," I said, "but there are no clean
glasses left in the living room."

"In the dining room cupboard there are clean glasses," my wife
said. She turned and looked at Ahmed through half-closed eyes.

She had never, as long as I could remember, looked at me like
that. Her eyes were always either wide open or completely shut, and
her eyelids never fluttered just for me.

"What are you waiting for?" my wife asked. "Didn't you hear me say there are glasses in the cupboard?"

"Maybe I should bring Ahmed something to drink," I said, "if he says what he'd like."

"Ahmed doesn't drink," my wife said.

There was no longer any reason to stick around. I headed toward the dining room. Along the way I plucked two grapes from a bowl sitting on the dishwasher. Before I left, I turned to look back. My wife and Ahmed were holding hands still. I could picture them in a flowery meadow with the huge orange orb of the sun sinking beyond the horizon. An evening breeze fluttered my wife's floral skirt and billowed Ahmed's green shirt. There were probably some birds in there, too. I imagined the bench I was sitting on while watching all this. Then I closed the kitchen door. "Where is my beer?" asked Haruki with a grin, and added that Hiroko had changed her mind, and she would have a little red wine. "Red wine is nice," said Haruki. "Like bitter chocolate," added Hiroko. There was a mirror at the back of the shelf, and when I reached for the glasses, I thought I might touch my face. It was the glasses, instead, that I touched: a tall straight one for Haruki, and one for wine, perched stork-like on one leg, for Hiroko. Both of them bowed at the same time, and turned to the table with the drinks. I closed the cupboard door and leaned toward the kitchen door. There was no sound.

***

Haruki and Hiroko came last to the party and I assume this was why they stayed longer than everyone else did. The act of bidding farewell by our front door took nearly half an hour. First we bowed to one another a few times, then Hiroko gave several compliments to the wine she had sipped then Haruki gave a five-minute congratulatory oration on the rolls my wife had prepared for the guests, then my wife twice recited the receipe for the fruit tart Hiroko had enjoyed, and Hiroko repeated it slowly back to her, claiming she would remember it and that she had a photogenic memory. "Photographic," said Haruki and bowed to her. "Yes," said Hiroko, "I have a photographic photogenic memory, and once I've heard something, no matter what it is, I never forget it." "How many eggs," I asked, "go into the cake?" "None," said Hiroko and bowed to me. "Maybe it is better if we shake hands," said my wife. She yawned and her teeth flashed in the light of the lamp over the door. Haruki took her proffered hand and bowed. "If we keep this up," I said, "we'll still be bowing at dawn. Good-night," I said and kissed Hiroko on the cheek.

We waited for their car to pull away and then we went into the house. Everywhere, on every available surface, there were glasses, small plates, crumpled napkins, trays and bowls. Chunks of roll crunched under foot. The bottles on the table were empty; there was only some of the vermouth left. I began to collect the glasses and plates and put them in the dishwasher. My wife went to the bathroom and a few minutes later I heard her brushing her teeth. Afterwards there was nothing to hear until she flushed the toilet. "Someone smoked weed in there," she said when she came back into the kitchen, "and forgot their joint on the edge of the tub."

"That's not fair," I said. "It is only decent to ask the host if he minds, and offer him the first hit."

"Maybe that is how it was back in your day," my wife said, "when there were other ways of doing things."

"Such as," I hurried to say, "that a wife holds hands with another man in front of her husband."

"I knew it," said my wife. "I can guess how that must have gnawed at you all evening. Come on, Ahmed is my student!"

"What is that supposed to mean," I asked, "I didn't see you holding hands with your other students."

"There wasn't time," she said.

"Of course there wasn't," I replied, "when you didn't let go of his hand even once."

"That's so not true," my wife protested. "Svetlana, my student from Russia, held his hand for awhile."

"Only one of them," I said, "his left, because you wouldn't relinquish his right."

"Do you mean to say," my wife said, "that you spent the whole evening obsessing about my hands? No wonder the guests felt you were neglecting them."

"If there was someone being neglected this evening," I said, "it was me."

"Next time I'll tell Ahmed to hold your hand," answered my wife, "maybe then you'll feel better."

She left the kitchen and went to the bedroom. I heard her click the lamp on the bedside table, turn down the bed spread and get ready to lie down. I waited for her to turn off the light, walked once more through the rooms where the guests had been, behind the potted cactuses I found two glasses and took them to the kitchen. I shook some food into a bowl for the cat, poured fresh water into another. I called, "Kitty," softly, "kitty, kitty." She didn't come. She had probably already crawled under the blanket, snuggled up to my wife and was sniffing her hands. I sat on a chair and lowered my head to the table. I leaned first my forehead on the table, then touched my left cheek to the smooth surface, then my right cheeck, and then I fell asleep.

***

When I opened my eyes, I saw my wife. She was sitting across from me, her hair tousled, and there was steam rising from the cup that was in front of her. I looked at the window and saw that it was already day.

"You spent the whole night here," my wife said, "as if you are homeless."

I shrugged, and winced at the ache in my stiff neck.

"I cannot believe," my wife said, "that you got so worked up about what was just a friendly little gesture."

"A friendly little gesture," I said, "that went on for hours." I meant my voice to sound snide, but it cracked and squeaked, as if my tongue couldn't maneuver my parched mouth.

"There is something you should know about Ahmed to help you understand," said my wife.

She clasped the cup with both hands, the way she did in wintertime, longing for warmth, or the way, of course, she had clasped Ahmed's hand the night before.

"Ahmed is from Iraq," my wife said, "and a few days ago he

learned that his sister and her children were killed in the bombing."

She looked me straight in the eyes.

I didn't know whether I could believe her. I asked, "How many children did she have?"

"Three," my wife said, and blinked. "That is why we decided," she continued, "that all of us would care for him, to help him deal with the loss." She smiled and raised the cup to her lips.

"What are you drinking?" I asked.

"Tea," said my wife. She licked her lips and set the cup on the table.

I reached out and and covered her hand, warm from the warmed cup, with mine. My wife sighed, softly, and then the two of us stared at our hands, pale in contrast to the dark surface of the table. I could feel the blood pulsing through one of them, but I wasn't sure which.

A little while later my wife slowly slipped her hand out and, without a word, brushed away the curls of hair that had slipped onto her face, got up and left the kitchen. I heard her open the wardrobe in the bedroom, probably looking for the clothes she would wear that day at school. I imagined her standing in front of the blackboard, writing out chemical formulas. Sitting at the desks behind her, the students are diligently copying everything from the blackboard into their notebooks. Only Ahmed is not writing. Instead he is staring at his open palm, as if reading his fate from the pale lines sketched across the darker skin.

I lifted my hand, picked up my wife's cup and had a sip of the tea. The tea was tepid and bitter from having steeped too long. It could use a few spoonfuls of sugar, I thought. I shifted my weight, drew my feet from under the chair, but I didn't get up. I saw the sugar bowl on the shelf over the stove, and the spoon was lying right by it. A step, maybe two, were all I'd need to reach them. I closed my eyes and slowly dropped my head to the table again. Somewhere inside me, somewhere very far off, I saw an airplane winging away, bombs dropping from under its wings, flaming tongues rising high into the air. I heard our front door open and shut. Then silence ruled the house. A while later the cat miaowed, but no matter how much I called to it and peered into all its hiding places, I couldn't find it.

MIROSLAVA DREAMED she was in a fragile boat being tossed to and fro in the waves, and when she woke with a start she saw she was in bed, next to Nikola, who was leaning on his left elbow while masturbating with his right hand. Miroslava squinted at the alarm clock: it wasn't even six. The bed kept rocking, and just in case she leaned over the edge to look and see whether they were, after all, on the surface of the sea. She could see the parquet floor, the crumbs and hairs, a crumpled-up business card, two coins and a hair clip, but nowhere, thank goodness, even a splash of water. She sighed with relief and sank back into her pillow, but then Nikola requested a tissue. Without opening her eyes, she stretched out a hand, groped for the package of tissues on her bedside table and passed it to Nikola. She could hear the paper crinkle, then Nikola's muffled moans. The bed shuddered once, and then all was still.

"Goodness," said Miroslava, "couldn't you have done that in the john?"

"There are some things better done in bed," answered Nikola and began whistling softly.

A little later the pages of a book rustled. Unlike Miroslava, he was never one to use a bookmark, and she thought that this time she had the right to gloat. At the same time she was bothered that she couldn't place the tune, and didn't know what book he was reading. What would she have been reading, she wondered, after masturbating? Love poems? Nikola had never in his life taken up a book of poetry, and he probably hadn't now; more likely, she thought, he'd picked up an adventure story, and now, relaxed and satisfied, he had given himself over to following the troubles plaguing the hero. Then Miroslava thought of the novels of Virginia Woolf, and she felt a tinge of sadness almost immediately: there was nothing so poignant as the image of a lonely woman who, after masturbating, read about the experiences of Mrs. Dalloway. She thought she might start to cry, but she mustn't allow herself that, so instead she sniffled loudly.

Nikola asked her if she wanted the tissue back. "Now it is your turn," he said and chuckled.

Miroslava reached out and opened her hand. I may never open my eyes again, she said to herself, and the thought scared her for a minute, then she felt the package of tissues touch her hand, and the touch brought her peace. She worked a tissue out, wiped her nose, crumpled it up and dropped it under the bed. She didn't hear anything, but she knew that the tissue had joined the hairs and crumbs, and she could imagine it resting with one tip on a coin, while it lay against the hair clip at its other end, ready to stay here forever or at least until the woman came who cleaned their apartment.

Nikola turned a page. A few minutes later he turned another, and soon afterwards the new page could be heard catching on the folds of the sheets.

"Don't skip ahead," said Miroslava grumpily. She squeezed her eyes shut while she spoke, and then there were real fireworks in the darkness behind her lids, just like a long time ago, she remembered, when she'd been little and pressed her thumbs against her closed eyes.

"I'm not skipping the story," said Nikola, "just the pictures."

"Don't be silly," said Miroslava. "They don't make novels these days with illustrations."

"Who," asked Nikola, "says I'm reading a novel?"

Miroslava rolled over toward him. If he was not reading a novel, what else could he be reading? She couldn't think of a single time he had picked up a book of essays; he despised memoirs because, he said, they were too long and packed with lies; he shuddered at philosophy, as well as at books on the natural sciences. Maybe she could open her eyes just a little, she thought, to see what Nikola was reading, but she gave up even before she tried peeking through her eyelashes. If she'd been able to stop from opening her eyes till now, then maybe she'd go ahead with them closed. She turned her head away to the other side, toward the window, and the darkness behind her eyelids thinned, as if they were becoming transparent. Soon, she knew, the rays of sunlight would be shining into the room, which would be the last warning that it was time to get up and start getting ready to go off to work.

Meanwhile Nikola had turned another page, abruptly, as if he were hurrying to follow the rhythm of some description or exciting twist in second-guessing the murder suspects.

I will never know, thought Miroslava as the darkness around her eyes grew lighter, but this time the certainty of that statement did not scare her at all. She tugged her nightgown down, raised the covers and put her feet on the floor. The floor was cold. Her slippers were here somewhere, but where? She inched her feet to the left and right, and after a few tries she felt the edge of one slipper under her toes. The other was right next to the first, though Miroslava had to lean over and figure out which one was for the left foot and which for the right. She slipped into them and got up and went off to the bathroom.

First she tried to picture the layout of the room, to figure out which route to take. Two steps, she thought, would bring her up next to the bed; then she should turn right, go around the chair with the clothes on it, take two or three more steps and that would get her to the hallway, then turn left, and then cross over to the bathroom, the door of which, she recalled, was always shut. The first two steps, however, were not enough, so that when she wanted to turn right, she walked into the bed frame and felt sharp pain ripple through her shin.

"What's this now," said Nikola, "can't a person read in peace in this house?"

Miroslava rubbed the sore place, groped for the edge of the bed and inched a little more to the left. If her calculations were correct, she was now in front of the door leading to the hallway, and all she had to do was watch out to step around the chair with the clothes on it at the right time. She put out her right hand, took two steps, and then stopped, uncertain. Where was the chair? she took another step, but still couldn't touch anything. Suddenly she thought that if she were to take even the smallest step, she would drop into an abyss, and she nearly opened her eyes. She could feel her heart pounding wildly, but at the same time she knew there was no turning back. She straightened up, dropped her arm and breathed deeply. She could take three more steps but didn't make it to the chair, and then she brushed the doorframe. Where was that chair? Had Nikola moved it the night before when he'd gotten undressed? There are things we will never know, she thought, shrugged her shoulders, and stepped into the hallway.

The bathroom was to the left of their room, at the end of the hallway. She figured it would take her four steps to get there with her eyes open, but this way, with her eyes shut, maybe she'd need five or six. At first she clutched the door frame, and then she pushed off from it and gave herself over to the air. She walked slowly, gingerly, though there was no furniture in the hallway, especially at that end, so she had no cause to worry about bumping into things. A coat tree and a telephone table stood by the front door to the right of their room, safely away from her back, though the feeling of certainty had no effect on the speed she moved. First she slid her left foot forward, then she drew her right foot to her left, leaned on both feet, and only then took the next step with her right foot, and then drew her left up to it. The doubling of steps confused her count; she was sure she had taken more than six steps but she wasn't yet across the hallway. She stopped and listened. There was no sound from their room. The soft humming from somewhere to the side must have been the refrigerator in the kitchen, across from their room, but when she tried to listen to it more closely and use it to position herself, the humming subsided. Miroslava stretched out both hands, but nowhere, in any direction, was there anything to touch. The darkness under her eyelids got thicker and darker, and she thought she ought to call Nikola to help her before the darkness swallowed everything up, and then she scolded herself for not opening her eyes and seeing where she was. In fact it was pretty strange that Nikola hadn't noticed anything while she shuffled through their room. He'd probably been so relaxed from masturbating that he'd fallen asleep with the book over his face, blessedly indifferent to what she was doing, especially this nonsense with her eyes being closed.

Of course, she could go back to their room, though that wouldn't change anything, except if she should decide to open her eyes, which was not what was on her mind. Again she thought that she would never open her eyes again, but this time she didn't feel scared. She would be leaving one world and settling into another, and the two worlds, despite the differences, would essentially be the same. She took a step with her left foot, then her right, then her left again, and then she ran into the door of the bathroom. She felt a surprisingly sharp pain in her toes and knee, so sharp, in fact, that she felt she was sure she'd broken her toe. On the other hand the blow stopped her movement and prevented her from running into the smooth surface of the door with her forehead and nose, which would most likely have resulted in heavy bleeding, and might have made her open her eyes. She groped for the doorknob, turned it and went into the bathroom, then carefully shut the door behind her, taking care not to slam it and wake up Nikola. By now she was convinced that he had drifted off into a deep sleep: had he been awake, he surely would have come to see what had made all the noise in the hallway. Maybe it's better this way, she thought, because then she would be able to come up with the best way of preparing him for her decision in peace and quiet, but first she had to do something which could no longer be postponed.

To the right of the door, at least that part was easy, was the toilet bowl. She pulled up her nightgown, sat down on the cold seat, and with a sigh of relief, she released a gush of urine. The bathroom was small, and when she got up, one step was enough to get her to the sink. There was a mirror right in front of her, and she tried to imagine her face in it. She couldn't. She turned to the small window, which looked out on the back yard, hoping that the additional light would thin the darkness beneath her eyelids and allow her to see her face somewhere inside her, but it didn't help. The best she could do was to summon some sort of empty face, which instead of the mouth and eyes had irregular holes, while there was a white patch where the nose was supposed to be. Only the ears were hers, and the locks of hair that curled next to her invisible cheeks.

She thought she might start crying, and then she changed her mind and pressed her temples with the tips of her fingers and for a few moments she held her breath. Then she found the faucet, turned it on, filled her cupped hands with water and splashed her face. Leaning over the sink, she waited for the drips to stop dripping, reached for a towel—she had always done this with her eyes closed anyway—dried her eyes, forehead and nose, and lifted her head again toward the mirror, but even then, despite her efforts, she couldn't summon a vision of what she looked like. Maybe she no longer had a face, she thought, and she felt a shiver slide down her spine. She shuddered, then she turned slowly, groped for the edge of the bathtub and sat down on it.

That is where she was sitting fifteen minutes later when Nikola came into the bathroom. She tried to explain to him what was happening, though she herself understood less and less of what it was she wanted to say. Meanwhile, Nikola kept demanding she open her eyes and stop acting like a dumb ass. He repeated those words time after time, placing emphasis first on one, then on another, and the more he repeated them, the more squeaky his voice became. The only time he fell silent was while he urinated, long and forcefully, so that the water and the urine must have sprayed all over the place, and Miroslava knew he was doing it to spite her, but she didn't say anything. She let him go on repeating, and his words soon turned to shouts, to howls, which prompted her to howl, and for a time they were shouting over one another, until finally he threatened to beat the shit out of her so bad she would never so much as blink, let alone play hide-and-go-seek or blind man's bluff, ever again.

"And you," said Miroslava, her voice suddenly calm, "would you hit a woman who can't see?"

Nikola's silence was a sure sign that she had startled him with the question. She could just see him blinking quickly, trying to muster any answer at all, and then tucking behind his back the hand that he had, without a doubt, raised to slap her.

"But," said Nikola, "you can see fine, it's just that you've decided not to."

"It doesn't matter how and why someone can't see," answered Miroslava, "what counts is the fact of the absence of sight. There are different ways to see, one doesn't see in only one way."

Nikola stopped talking again, and Miroslava knew that she had almost gotten him cornered. She did not, however, know what would happen then, but there was no hurry. Sooner or later, as it always happens, things would take their true place, and all the earlier effort would turn out to be wasted.

Nikola spoke up, "It's all because of that, isn't it?" Miroslava didn't understand right away what he had in mind, but then the memory stirred in her of the rocking boat, and Nikola's hand moving up and down his red penis. The storm in her dream had been so wild! While the boat had rocked and creaked, her one thought had been tied to dying, to the *despair* that she would die and become fish food at the bottom of some lake or a sea and she wouldn't even know what it was called. That was why she was indifferent when she saw the reason why the bed was shaking: there was no penis stronger than death or that could at least serve as a life raft for the shipwrecked. In any other situation, she would surely have leaned over and given Nikola a hand in finishing the job, but with her mouth full of fear that possibility was simply out of the question.

"Let me be perfectly clear," she said, "I have nothing against your penis, or masturbation, I regret that I will never see it again, however, my decision not to see has nothing to do with what you were doing in bed."

"In other words," said Nikola, "from here on in you are not interested in how the world looks."

"No," said Miroslava, "I am not interested in how the world looks. I have already seen it plenty of times."

"And me," continued Nikola in a softer voice, "what about with me?"

"What with you?"

"Aren't you interested in what I look like?"

Miroslava tried to summon his face, and quickly somewhere in the uneven darkness under her eyelids, she could see his eyes, cheeks, bushy mustache, the mole on his left nostril, quite nicely. Then she tried to imagine herself, and once again she was faced with an empty place in the shape that was supposed to be her face. It isn't fair, she thought, it really isn't fair, and out loud she said, "I know what you look like, I don't need to see you each time all over again."

Nikola said nothing. Then she heard him turn the doorknob, open the door, and go out into the hallway. Miroslava sharpened her ears, but she couldn't tell which direction he was headed, until she heard the dial jangling on the telephone as it turned. Silence followed, then Nikola explained to someone that he was Miroslava Atanacković's husband, and that he was calling her to let them know she wouldn't be coming to work. Then there was a new silence, when the person he was talking to probably asked for the reason why she'd be out. Something has lodged in her eye, said Nikola, and he added that he would be taking her to the eye clinic straight away. Then he stopped talking again, and then finally in a soft voice he said he would certainly let them know what the doctors decided. "Now she can't see anything," he said at the end, "but that probably won't last too long."

He set the receiver down almost soundlessly. If Nikola was angry, thought Miroslava, he wasn't showing it. She imagined the cradle on the phone, the receiver in it, and the cord, twisted and tangled, and then she imagined Nikola's fingers separating from the phone, and how his fingers, and whole hand, rose to his forehead, how they came down on it and pressed and rubbed it, as if that might help, as if what had happened were just a drawing done with a pencil that could be erased. "Nothing can be erased," she whispered, and then she began imagining her lips, teeth and tongue moving as they formed sounds, letters, words. She wanted to imagine her ear, and the eardrum membrane that vibrated while the receiver was in the cradle, while the words were circling around the room, but she gave up, because she wasn't sure how the ear looked inside, and how the vibrating of the membrane turns into information about the sound. She would have to read about that, she thought, in the medical encyclopedia, and then she remembered that she couldn't see, so books were no longer available to her, and that she would be forced, if she really wanted to learn something, to ask Nikola to read to her. Instantly she imagined them sitting at the kitchen table: Nikola reading news from the paper, and she listening, her head cocked slightly to the side, and sometimes, only seldom, she would ask him for an additional explanation. She imagined herself from behind so that she wouldn't have to fret over the empty place on her face, and she imagined Nikola with blue eyes, different from his real eyes, but the eyes she had always wished she could see on his face. At last, she thought, at last the world will be the way I want it to be. She clapped her hands, thrilled, and called to Nikola.

"Nikola," she shouted, "where are you? I have something important to tell you."

Nikola did not answer.

Miroslava stretched out her hand, touched the door frame, took two small steps and came out into the hallway.

The apartment was silent. There were no sounds coming from anywhere, not from a single room: the parquet floor didn't creak, there was no gurgle of water, no hum of the refrigerator, no clatter of plates, no ringing voice of a television anchorperson. If he was in the apartment, Nikola wasn't budging. He was crouched somewhere, thought Miroslava, sure that this is a whim of mine that will pass. She wanted to shout out that it wasn't like that, that he was wasting his time thinking this was something temporary, and that he would be better off getting used to it straight away, but then she felt something touched her shoulder. She turned quickly, thrust out her hand and waved it every which way, until she thought she felt a touch to the back of her head. Then she spun around again, swinging wildly with her right hand and the swing spun her yet again, and soon she no longer knew whether she was facing the front door or the bathroom door. She was breathing fast, her heart pounding, her hands shook, her knees buckled. She wanted to tell Nikola to stop teasing, but she couldn't form the words. The fear that had started to fill her was unlike anything else; all she could do was follow it as it mushroomed, turning into sheer horror, into something that eluded any attempt to describe it. She opened her mouth, choking on a lack of air, and then she heard the dull thud of footsteps. They were coming from far off, no rush, no impatience, comfortable that they were headed in the right direction and that there was nothing that would stop them. Miroslava felt beads of sweat drip down her ears, down her neck, all the way to her collar bone. The steps meanwhile became firmer, closer, heavier; the floor under them rocked like water, and Miroslava suddenly felt as if she were in a boat again, on a tossing sea, among the waves. Even if she had wanted to flee, she wouldn't have been able to. The footsteps by then had come very close. Miroslava raised her hands in front of her. She stood that way for awhile, and when the steps stopped, she dropped her hands.

For three months now there has been a sign in our neighbor's front yard advertising that the house is for sale. This is the house of our neighbors to the left. The house on the right was recently renovated, so they certainly are not thinking of selling it, at least not for now. The house to the left, however, has seen better days, and this is the main reason, or so my wife thinks, that they have not been able to find a buyer for such a long time, though our papers are repeating day in and day out that the available real estate in Calgary is not enough to meet the vast demand. Every two or three days an agent from a real estate agency brings around people who are looking for a new home, but we are already into the fourth month that the house is for sale, and the sign is still there, unchanged.

It doesn't bother me. I even find it engaging to observe the potential buyers from behind the curtain, their bold stride and grinning faces as they get out of their cars and follow the agent, and their plodding stride and glowering expressions after they have finished touring the house and go back to their neatly parked cars. There are sometimes children with them, and a dog. The children run, call to each other, make noise, and the dog, just in case, starts marking the new territory and leaving its spoors.

"I don't get it," I said one day to my wife when new buyers arrived on the neighbor's lawn with their dog, "why do people take a dog along with them and not a cat when they are looking at a house. Don't cats care where they will live?"

"You'd be advised," my wife said while she peered over my shoulder, "to start thinking about what we'll do if a family moves in with little kids. It'll be easy with the dogs, that is our least worry."

My wife does not hate children, she simply does not like to have them in her immediate vicinity. She told me so as soon as we met. Then I didn't care; later I hoped she'd have a change of heart; afterwards I learned that there are some things a person cannot hope for. When we bought our house, after all, my wife demanded that there be no children in the houses on either side of us, on both sides of the street. That is why we settled on this neighborhood, where most of the residents were retired. After a while, some of the retirees died, others went to homes for the elderly, and now children of various ages could be often seen and heard. Our part of the street, until recently, according to my wife, was the last haven of peace and quiet, but now, to her horror, this haven is being threatened with the danger that it may disappear.

First, as soon as the sign announcing the sale went up, she called our lawyer to ask whether she could forbid the sale of the house to families with little kids. The lawyer informed her that she could sell her own home to anyone she wanted, she had no need for a formal prohibition, but when my wife explained that she wasn't calling about our house, but about the house of our neighbors to the left, the lawyer asked to speak to me. I listened patiently to his complaint, during which he informed me of how many times my wife had called him the last two weeks. "Twelve times," said the lawyer "and her demands included suing your supermarket for rotten potatoes, seeking a ban on bringing young children in public transport, reporting the woman from a nearby street because the grass was too long in her back yard, and yesterday she insisted that I write into your will that the funeral must not be held in the rain."

"Whose funeral?" I asked.

"Yours," said the lawyer. "Her funeral is not even mentioned in the will."

I said nothing to my wife. After all, when she decides something, there is no force powerful enough to prevent her. "Did she make plans," I asked the lawyer, "for where I would be buried?"

"You will be cremated," the lawyer answered, "and then she is taking the urn to Belgrade, where there will be a memorial service."

"And that is when it shouldn't be raining?"

"Right," said the lawyer, "the day must be beautiful."

"Wasn't I smart to think of that?" my wife said proudly when I complained to her about this. "That way no one will get mud on their clothes or shoes, not like back at Bežanija cemetery when they buried my aunt during a downpour. My poor uncle slipped and sat down in the mud," she said, "and our godfather got his shoe stuck in his galoshes and he almost couldn't find it. After all," said my wife, "it will be nicer for you, too, in the sun than in the rain."

That's true. I have hated the rain ever since I can remember. I called the lawyer and said that I agreed with my wife's request regarding the funeral. The lawyer sighed and hung up the phone without a word.

Meanwhile, my wife had come up with a new strategy for the people considering the house of our neighbors to the left. She found a "Beware of Dog!" sign and added the words "The Dog Bites!" to it in red lettering, and then she hung the sign up on the low fence that separated our front yard from the neighbor's.

Two days later, a young married couple got out of a brand-new van and went over to the neighbor's house. By the hand the wife was leading a little boy who had only just learned how to toddle, but the moment she caught sight of the sign on the fence, she swept the boy up, spun around, and while her husband ran after her, she fled back to the van. Her husband tried to convince her to get out, but then he got into the van, and soon they were gone.

The next day the neighbor knocked at our door. My wife asked me not to open it to him, and when I refused and started walking toward the door, she locked herself in the bathroom.

"What is this?" asked the neighbor. "Since when have you had a dog?" He was holding my wife's sign.

"We don't have it any more," I said. "It was biting, so we returned it to its previous owner."

My neighbor shoved the sign furiously into my hands, looked me up and down in a rage, and marched out of the yard.

My wife came out of the bathroom and said that she was proud of me. She wanted to call the lawyer immediately and submit a request for compensation for suffering and fear. She had had to sit down on the toilet, she explained, because her legs were shaking so badly, and her heart, look, was still pounding. I told her to lie down, and, just to be safe, I unplugged the phone.

After that my wife changed her tactics. She found a horrendous old hag mask at a store, probably left over from Halloween, and then, whenever she caught sight of potential buyers with small children, she'd put the mask on. The mask had a knobby nose with several revolting warts, protruding teeth and long, gray, matted hair. My wife would wait for the buyers to go into the neighbor's house, then she'd put on a shabby house dress, grab a broom and go out into the back yard. She wouldn't do anything special in the yard, she'd just stand there in the corner of the back porch, easily visible from the kitchen of our neighbors to the left. Sooner or later, someone would come to the window—people are sure to be interested in the view from the kitchen, especially if there is a sink nearby—and catch sight of my wife, and then there would be a fuss and a panic, and you could see the frightened people through the neighbor's window as they gesticulated and quarreled. All of that with the audible cries and sobs of children.

This time the neighbor didn't come knocking, he called the police. The police car pulled in and parked in front of our house on Wednesday afternoon. The policeman who rang was young. He smiled when I opened the door and said that they'd received a report that a mentally disturbed woman lived here who was putting on masks and attacking children.

"Nonsense," I said, "my wife wouldn't hurt a fly. She was trying on that costume," I added, "to get ready for Halloween."

"Halloween is six months away," the policeman said.

"My wife is a perfectionist," I answered.

The policeman was insistent. He asked if he could see her.

"She has gone off to a game of bingo," I said. "She plays bingo every Wednesday, but she never wins anything."

The policeman said that he played Lotto, but he, too, had never won anything. He asked to see her costume. "I assume," he said, "that she hasn't worn it to play bingo?"

I asked him to wait. I went up to the room, put on the mask, wrapped the shabby house dress around me and grabbed the broom. When I appeared suddenly in front of the policeman, he was startled and his hand flew to his gun. "Hey," he said, "that is one dangerous mask." He reached over and fingered the wart on the nose. He sniffed his fingers. "They seem almost real," he said, "they even smell of pus."

"The hair is real, too," I replied, "it isn't synthetic."

The police rubbed some of the hairs between his fingers. He said that the mask would appeal to his wife, and he asked where we'd gotten it. He took out a pad and jotted down the name of the shop. While he was writing, over his shoulder I noticed our neighbor: he was wiping the For Sale sign with a damp cloth. By that time the policeman had written down the address, tucked his pad into his shirt pocket, said goodbye and left. As the police car pulled away, I saw a new van pull up to the neighbor's house, and out of it came a husband an wife, three small children and two dogs. I closed the door and hurried to the back porch. The bathrobe tripped me up, but still I got out onto the back porch just as the faces of the young married couple appeared in the kitchen window. A little later they were joined by the face of our neighbor. All three of them stared at me, their eyes bulging. At first I felt a little awkward, and then I remembered my wife, and slowly, ever so slowly, I raised the broom in greeting.

ALEXANDER COHEN had been feeling lately that his wife was more distant with each day, as if she were on her way down a polished slide. He remembered how he had taken Sarah to a playground twenty years before and let her go down a slide just like that: he climbed up to the top with her, set her at the start, showed her how to hold her legs, and his wife waited at the bottom of the curving path, prepared to grab her before she plunked into the sand. How long could that journey have been? Three-four meters? Not even. But Alexander Cohen clearly remembered the horror he had felt as Sarah slid away. Each time he felt she was leaving forever and he was close to tears as he clambered back down the metal steps, listening to Sarah's elated shouts in her mother's arms. It was worst for him when she turned around one time, halfway down, where the curve began after which he wouldn't be able to see her any more and waved back at him. He thought his heart would burst, and a little later, when he went over to the spot, his legs shaking, where his wife had hugged Sarah, he was certain he would never survive it when his daughter really left home.

When she did, he was not even there to say goodbye. Her leave-taking had actually begun earlier, because for months before she left she had been staying with the boy she was seeing. That evening was when she was moving out for good so that she could live with him, and the day before she had rejected every proposal her parents made for her to wait until the two of them married. "Who is talking about marriage here?" she shouted before she slammed the door. Alexander Cohen listened patiently the next day to his wife who was trying to get him to stay home and he explained that he had to go off on his duty rounds. His wife was certain that between the two of them they would be able to convince Sarah to change her mind, but Alexander Cohen was unrelenting. He went off on his duty rounds, and from that day forward his wife began to distance herself from him, at first almost imperceptibly, then faster and faster, until the speed with which she slid away reminded him of that slide in the children's playground, across the street from their house.

He went over to the window and looked out. The playground was still in the same place, but the slide Sarah used to go down on was gone. Instead he saw a plastic slide, designed to look like a castle, with fortified walls and a guard tower. He would never have taken Sarah to that castle, that much he knew, because the big plastic plaything reminded him irresistibly of a prison. Sarah had felt free on the old slide, polished by all the little rear ends that had slid down it. A few times, flinging her arms wide, she had shouted, "I am a bird. I am a butterfly. I am a sparrow." She would never have said that if she had been going down a slide like the one that was in the playground now. What could she shout as the slide took her down into the depths of the castle, to the dungeon? He ought to give her a call, tell her she was lucky to have been born at the right time for the right kind of slide, but then he remembered that her boyfriend might pick up the phone and he instantly lost all interest in calling her. What was the young man's name? He couldn't recall, though he wasn't even sure he had ever heard the name; he had seen him, as far as he could remember, only once. It was a Sunday, boring like every Sunday, and Alexander Cohen had opened the door to Sarah's room without knocking, thinking she wasn't home. He was looking for the paper, interested in seeing what movies were on; instead, he saw her boyfriend, completely naked. The boy was standing in the middle of the room, motionless, no shred of shame, as if waiting to hear what Alexander Cohen would say. Cohen said nothing; instead he coughed and slowly closed the door, though later he had to admit that for those seconds he mostly stared at the boy's half-erect member, wondering to himself, then and later, whether it was possible that this appendage had been inside his daughter's body. Then he was consumed by rage and he had to leave the apartment, alarmed by the fury that grew in him with incredible speed; now, however, he felt only sorrow and a kind of numbness, which he could put no name to.

Years ago he would have told his wife all about it, just as he had told her all his dreams and everything he experienced. There were some things he told her several times, especially what had transpired with the unknown woman on the crowded bus. It just so happened that when she was pressed by people who were elbowing to get on board, the woman had leaned back against him, her bottom rubbing his underbelly. The bus began to move, and while everyone was swaying and pushing, Alexander Cohen felt his member rise, stiffen. He tried pulling away from the woman, but his body came up against an unmoving wall of other bodies, and then he felt that the woman was actually nudging in closer to him, slowly moving her bottom into place, until his member was lying in the crack between her buttocks. "Did you come?" asked his wife every time when he came to that part, and he always said he hadn't, though in fact he had, indeed, come, which led the woman in front of him to stop fidgeting, and she quickly got off the bus, perhaps at the very next stop. In his story, the ride lasted a few more stops, all the way to the city park, where they got off together, she going right and he going left.

"You are crazy," his wife told him, "you should have followed her. I would have."

"You as you?" he asked her, "Or you if you were a man?"

"Me as me," answered his wife. "Why should I have to become a man?"

Alexander Cohen had no answer for that, just as he had no answer for the question of why his wife was getting more distant. Some questions, he consoled himself, would always be left unanswered, but that was no comfort when he went to bed at night and felt the void that divided him from his wife, who was lying all the way over on the far side of the bed. He didn't even try lying closer to her, for fear that she might get up and go to another bed. At least this way he could hear her breathing and hope that, if she slept restlessly, she might stretch an arm or leg out as she slept and touch him. She slept motionlessly, however, and he had to wonder whether she ever had bad dreams. No one, he told himself, can have only good dreams, sooner or later there has to be a nightmare, and then she'd turn to him as if he were the only person who could shield her from the evil that was making her teeth chatter. But he waited in vain and fought to stay awake: the nights passed and she never budged, indeed it seemed to him that she was sleeping partly off the edge of the bed, floating midair, like a woman whom a hypnotist has made as stiff as a board.

"Don't you ever dream anything?" he asked her one morning. It was Saturday, they were sitting in the living room, having coffee and reading the newspaper. Actually she was the only one reading the paper; his face was so swollen from lack of sleep that he could barely see out from under his puffy eyelids.

"Me?" she asked, as if there were at least a dozen people in the living room. "Whatever's gotten into you? I never stop dreaming. From the moment I lie down, until morning comes and I open my eyes, I live in one gorgeous dream."

"Really?" he asked. "What makes it so gorgeous?"

She looked at him, frowning; she looked at him for a long time until he was regretting having spoken to her at all. "I think you'd rather not hear," she said, finally.

He was persistent, but not very: he repeated two or three times that she really ought to tell him. Then he stopped asking and watched her as her lips moved ever so slightly while she read. They didn't move all the time, sometimes they were quiet, pursed, as if at rest.

"I won't say," said his wife, without looking up.

"I know," he said. He had nothing left to do there; he got up and went into the bathroom to shave. The skin on his face was tired, sagging, and he looked to himself like one of those melting clocks of Dali's. The razor snagged, leaving bloody nicks, and when he'd finished shaving he felt worse than when he'd started. His wife was still sitting in the living room, staring at the paper. Alexander Cohen thought maybe he ought to say something to her, but he couldn't think of what except that the skin on his neck was stinging him something terrible, and that, he knew, his wife wasn't interested in hearing.

So he went back to bed, which he hadn't done for nearly thirty years. When he woke up it was noon. Silence reigned in the apartment, no, it was the ticking of the large wall clock that reigned; time seemed to be strolling from room to room, from the kitchen to the bathroom, and back. Alexander Cohen turned to look at the other side of the bed but there was no one there. He had expected, for no reason, to see his wife there, but all he saw were her pyjamas, tossed carelessly over the pillow. If she was in the apartment at all there was no sound to suggest her presence, which made Alexander Cohen try to keep as quiet as possible as he got up and dressed. At one moment while he was pulling a T-shirt over his head and found himself in a transparent twilight, it occurred to him that perhaps something had happened to her, maybe she had slipped in the bathtub or had had a stroke, but he immediately pushed the thought away. Nevertheless, while getting dressed, he cautiously opened the bathroom door, moving it slowly, as if he was expecting to stumble over an inert body on the tiled floor. The bathroom was empty, as was the living room, and there was no one on the terrace. He stepped outside, leaned over the railing and looked into the yard: it was empty, if he didn't count the striped cat, basking in the sun. All that was left was the kitchen, but he would need the most time for the kitchen. He waited until he felt sweat dripping down his temples, and then slowly, moving sideways, crab-like, he crossed the hallway and, covering his eyes with his hand, stepped into the kitchen.

The kitchen, too, was empty like all the other rooms. There were coffee cups drying on a plastic rack. Next to them, also clean, were saucers, teaspoons and a coffee pot. The only thing he couldn't see was the sugar bowl. He considered going back to the living room to look for it there, and then, as he was turning, he noticed the sheet of paper on the table. He went over, picked it up and brought it up to his face. There was a single sentence on it, written in letters of varying size: *I've never loved you.* He read it once again, and then turned the sheet of paper over and looked at the other side. He was hoping when he turned it back there wouldn't be anything written on it, but the sentence was still where it had been, and probably, thought Alexander Cohen, where it would be forever. He pulled back a chair, sat down and placed the sheet of paper on the table. If nothing else, at least he knew why the dream his wife had mentioned was so wonderful —because he wasn't in it. He reached out and took hold of the piece of paper with the message that his wife had written on it. Maybe he should read it once again, he thought. Instead, he crumpled it up, tore off a piece, put it in his mouth and started chewing.

"LET'S TALK about love," says my wife. She says this as if a conversation about love is the simplest thing on earth, as if it is enough for our eyes to meet across a table, a candle flame, perhaps, and then the words will start to flow as easily as a river, or, at least, a swollen stream. But, what do we really, I mean *really*, know about love? If she had suggested we speak of trigonometry or palatalization, or hydraulic presses, I'd have had more to say, I might even have sketched something, there might have been room for a poem, but love left me mute, groping for the right words, or even the wrong words, in fact the wrong words more than the right ones, because the skill of speaking implies the use of both, and a well-composed speech is based on pointing out the wrong words which, if used, would definitely ruin such a fine speech.

My wife, however, is still calm. "I don't see," she says, "what that has to do with love and why you are saying all these things. You always," she says, "try to make the simple complicated, and turn something ordinary into something murky and tangled."

"If you mean to say," I reply, "that love is simple and ordinary, then we really have nothing to discuss."

"You already wrote that sentence in a story," says my wife. "We'd agreed there would be no repetition."

"Love is repetition," I say, "which cannot be said for my sentence, but even if it could, the sentence would stand. One best speaks of repetition," I say triumphantly, "by repeating."

"I hate you," says my wife. And then quickly adds, "I have never said that to you before."

She gives the additional sentence as if with remorse, but, as far as I know, remorse is not typical of her, so I'd be wise to be cautious. All these years, ever since she first turned up in my stories, my wife has been reliable in only one regard: her lack of reliability, and that, I believe, is what makes her so appealing to readers, especially women, who are convinced that my wife is the ideal spouse for a writer, particularly someone as insecure and fickle as I am. I muse on all of this in code, of course, because ever since the first story, my wife has been reading not only my texts, as many readers know, but also my thoughts.

"That's exaggeration," says my wife. "Once or twice it just so happened that I said aloud exactly what you were thinking. It was a coincidence which can be quantified with a given percentage of probability and it could happen to anyone. Even you," she says.

"There you go again reading my mind," I answer, "yet you didn't count that instance as one of the coincidences you allege. How, then, can I believe you?"

"Fine," says my wife, "so it happened three times. The third time was just now. Satisfied?"

I say nothing. I should be satisfied, but recently I have been beset by an indifference which elbows out any satisfaction. The indifference is not for my wife (never could I be indifferent to her) nor is it for my stories (they still set fires burning in me), but for a world that no longer stirs me. I have stopped going out. I do not look out of the window. I do not turn on the television. I do not answer the phone. Sometimes I jot down a sentence, but only a short one. I crumble cookies into warm milk in the morning and evening, and afterward carefully pick all the crumbs off the table cloth, while for lunch I eat everything my wife puts in front of me. I haven't even been reading. I read the last book a year ago, and I don't remember the author, or the title, or even the picture on the cover.

"I knew the story wasn't about me," my wife says. "As soon as you're supposed to be talking about love, you come up with a hundred reasons for talking about something else. Who cares about your indifference, anyway?"

My wife's rudeness, now that would be something to write about, but I'll leave it for a more opportune moment. I can't talk about my indifference either, because I am indifferent to it. So all I have left is love, despite the anxiety, despite the shipwrecked words that have plagued my travels until now in the sphere of love.

"What sphere," asks my wife, "what are you talking about? Love is not a ball or a balloon, nor is it a prism or a pyramid. Drop the geometry and like abstractions. Love is concrete."

She utters the last sentence with unconcealed pride, as if she has just discovered the meaning of the existence of the universe. She is wrong, however, if she thinks she can rattle my indifference and sweep it under the rug.

"It's awful," declares my wife, "that you can even write something like this! When I clean," she says, "I clean, I do not sweep the rubbish under the carpet. Someone will end up thinking I am slovenly and so negligent. There," she says, lifting the corner of the rug. "Tell me, is there anything else to see under here, but the flooring?"

"No," I must confess, "there is nothing there but the flooring, not even a speck of dust." This would, perhaps, be a convenient moment to change the subject, but I don't know why I began this story, nor how my wife and I turned up in it.

My wife, who has been down on her knees all this time straightening the tassels on the rug, looks up suddenly, and asks, incredulous, "You mean to say you don't know how to get us out of this story? Can't we go out the same way we came in?"

"If I knew the way," I say, "I wouldn't merely go back, I would begin again."

"So," says my wife, "we'll be stuck here forever."

"Yes," I say.

"You could at least have written a nice sentence," my wife says. "I like being in a nice sentence. Nice and long."

I say nothing, I don't answer. My wife says nothing, either. This is not the first time we have sat together in silence, but we are sitting this time in an ominous silence. It is not easy to get used to the idea that we will never step out of these sentences, that we will be stuck in one, out of all the possible stories, where nothing happens.

"Is there bread anywhere?" asks my wife.

"Where would bread fit," I answer with a question, "in a story about love?"

"Love won't sustain you, dear," says my wife. "You should have mentioned a refrigerator at the beginning of the story and filled it with fifteen days worth of food. By then somebody would probably find us."

"Don't be so sure," I say. "Stories haven't many readers these days.

If we were in a novel, someone might leaf through it, but as things stand we have nothing to hope for in a story."

"Novel or story," my wife replies angrily, "I don't care. I'm hungry for my own sake, not the reader's." Then her face lights up. "This is your story," she says. "All you need to do is describe a loaf of bread, and there you are." She claps her hands in delight, then stops, tilts her head to the side, and adds, "And white cheese spread, too."

"You mean *kajmak* cheese spread?"

"Yes, describe *kajmak*, too," my wife explains impatiently. "There's nothing finer than bread and *kajmak*. But take care: the bread should be warm, and the *kajmak* shouldn't be aged."

I do not answer, at least not right off. First I imagine warm bread, a good crust, cracked on top, and I add the paddle with the long handle that the baker uses to take the loaf of bread from the oven. "Good," I think, "that was easy, but how do I describe the *kajmak*?"

"You are the writer," says my wife. "Don't look at me."

I explain to her that somewhere I read how *kajmak* is made only in Serbia and Bulgaria, so there is no point to describing something with which most of humanity is entirely unfamiliar.

"I knew this would happen," replies my wife, "and that you'd be blaming humanity for your writer's block."

I make no effort to stand up for myself. Her words are not far from the truth: when I make a mistake I always say it is someone else's fault because I am simply never wrong. And now, when I should be admitting that I don't know how to find the way out of this story that I so readily, with no forethought, dropped us into, I stand on my tiptoes in hopes of catching sight of a reader who might show us the way instead of starting at the right hand margin and seeking an opening in a word parsed into syllables.

Meanwhile my wife is digging in earnest. She has taken the baker's paddle, shortened the handle, and now she is focused on digging a hole in the sand. I have no idea where the sand came from, but my wife has raised her finger to her lips, and then whispers that I shouldn't say a word. "If I doubt the sand," she says, "who knows what will come to take its place, though this paddle has its limits. While the sand is here, there is hope that a way out to somewhere else will be possible, maybe from a passage in the middle of the story, at a moment when no one is thinking of the conclusion."

As usual, my wife is right. All we need to do is wait for a sufficiently inattentive reader and then, when the reader's mind wanders, we'll slip out between sentences, like a newborn in an easy birth.

"There you go again talking nonsense," says my wife. "No such thing as an easy birth. I could forgive you the *kajmak*, but I'm sick of men who mess with women's subjects. What do you," she asks, "know about giving birth? Have you ever tried?"

I keep my mouth shut because I know where this is headed: a lecture on women's literature and the inability of men to write of the world of women in a credible way. "Here," says my wife, "how do I come across in your stories? A witch and a grouch. And you," she continues, "how do you portray yourself? As a powerless yet well-intentioned guy whose wife does not allow him to express himself freely. If this story were being written by a woman," my wife shouts, "you'd get what's coming to you!"

"I told you nicely we shouldn't talk about love," I say in a calm voice, "but you wouldn't listen."

"If you really think love is measured in different ways inside the story and outside of it," says my wife, "then I definitely will not leave. I will hide behind a verb and no one will find me."

"It won't help," I say, smiling, "because a true reader reads behind the words and between the lines."

"We'll see about that," says my wife and disappears.

I don't look for her. There are too many verbs behind me, it would be a hopeless task. And besides, the end of the story is in sight. I'll sit down, on this word here, yes, right here, in this sentence and wait. Once she's eaten all the bread, she'll come looking for me, and she might come back before that, when it gets dark. My wife is afraid of the dark, so I'll ask the reader to switch on a light, at the very least a small table lamp, while reading this story. And afterwards if the reader could bring a glass of water. Bread gets easily caught in the throat, particularly when it's dry.

No, no, and no, no matter how hard he tried, no matter what he did, Mileta Micić could not accept the notion that the world would go on being there after his death. The thought that the very next morning after he died the sun would rise again in the east, that newspaper kiosks and grocery stores would open and city buses would rumble down shady streets, children would go to school and adults to work, that this would be a day, in a word, like any other, this thought cast him into despair. No, no, and no, he repeated to himself, everything cannot simply come to an end in such a way, that he would leave almost by stealth from the great world stage, as if we are nothing more than extras in our own lives, extras who slip out of a hidden side door, while on stage creatures remain cocooned, mummified, which suddenly claim to know all there is to know about us, in more detail and better than we know ourselves.

No, no, and no, Mileta Micić refused to accept this and nothing could sway him. There was also nothing, of course, that might confirm the possibility that he was right after all, no statement by any witness had been preserved anywhere, a statement to confirm, for instance, that someone, anyone, had come back to the stage, regardless of which door he'd left by. If there was someone who had been in the other world and had come back from there—not counting, of course, the heroes of myth—then the one, this one who did come back, had either forgotten it all, or had been banned from speaking of it. Mileta Micić immediately dismissed the latter possibility because a ban means nothing to members of the human race. He had seen countless times that the more vigorously a ban was imposed, the greater the likelihood it would be violated. Forgetting was something else and he could imagine visitors from the other world, the world of the dead, or rather those who had been permitted to return to the first world, the world of the living, crossing through a scanner of sorts at the border which would erase their memories, especially those having to do with their time spent in the other world.

No, no, and no, Mileta Micić fretted, it could not be so simple.

Life is more tangled than that, after all, and it does not resolve by simply crossing a border. Besides, who ever said there was a border zone between this here and that there, anyway? And what if these worlds are actually intermingled and partially overlap, so that there are dead among the living and vice versa? Seen from that angle, Mileta Micić mused that maybe his dilemmas were pointless, perhaps he had already been dead for a long time? If he was dead, how to be sure? Pinch himself? He pinched himself and yelped with pain. Good, he thought, he was alive. If he'd been dead, it wouldn't have hurt, for sure, and he also probably wouldn't have yelped. If the dead speak, he thought, they speak in deep voices. Even children who died prematurely, whose voices hadn't changed yet, even they spoke in deep voices.

No, no, and no, Mileta Micić warned himself, things can't possibly be like that! What was he thinking, he wondered, and where did he get this idea about life being like a horror movie? Life is more beautiful than that. Much more beautiful; with this assertion he would always agree, regardless of the fact that agreeing with it brought him so much pain and anxiety. If life were not beautiful, and the world were not beautiful, everything would be much easier. All it took was the thought of the magnificent structure of nature, the animal and plant kingdom, and then imagining that he would never see this ever again, and everything came tumbling down around him, he even tumbled down inside himself out of pure despair, out of his inability to influence things in any way. He could always, of course, wonder about the meaning of life, but no, no, and no, he said to himself a thousand times that he would not make such ridiculous mistakes. To wonder about the meaning of life is absurd while a person is living, since meaning surely lies in part in the very act of living. In other words, the meaning of life is life itself, or, should he want to be more precise, the meaning of life is in restoring death. One lives to die. That did not have the ring of a slogan likely to enjoy widespread popularity, thought Mileta Micić, but—if this is any comfort—the truth is never popular, is it?

Recently, Mileta Micić recalled, he had read a short story by a fellow writer from our part of the world in which the writer said that the meaning of life was contained in love. How stupid, what a measure of credulity! Because, if there is something incapable of serving as a vehicle for the meaning of life, that would be love. How could such an unreliable emotion, so fickle and subject to the most varied influences, be banner-bearer in the caravan of meaning? No, no, and no, Mileta's entire organism rebelled, there is no place here for love, never has been, never will be. Love is transient, shamelessly selfish and easily replaceable, and therefore it cannot be what spurs a person not to believe in an end to life, the moment after which a person is no longer the way he was until that moment, a moment when we all become something else, no one knows exactly what, just as no one knows what happens at the very beginning, how a person becomes a person, where consciousness comes from and whether it later disappears to or has—as Mileta Micić had long been sensing—a manifold role, i.e. arriving with one person, leaving with that person, then coming back with another, without a word about where it had been and where it might go again.

No, no, and no, Mileta Micić smacked his right fist onto the open palm of his left hand, he would not give up so easily, he would not allow life to leave him to the mercy and mercilessness of death and he would show life who's in charge here, even though—when he had thought about it—it wasn't clear why he had it in for death when all death was seeking was whatever life had already done. It's not the arrival of death that makes a person die, but the departure of life, right? It's all life's fault, the birthing and the dying, the mocking duration after it has used you and discarded you like a plastic bag with a hole in it. He liked the image and he could clearly envision himself walking along, his legs far apart because of the largish hole on the plastic bag he was wearing. The bag was large and hung on him, and through the hole at the bottom his pendulum could be seen swinging in all four directions, exactly as he had once read in *Till Eulenspiegel*. He smiled wistfully when he remembered the books he had read in his erstwhile youth, but the melancholy brought him no relief, because at the same moment he thought of how people would be reading those same books when he was no longer there and he felt fury, and even ground his teeth.

No, no, and no, he cautioned himself again, he mustn't allow anger to gain the upper hand. A calm mind sleeps longer, he recited to himself and then asked himself what it was, really, that angered him in this fury of his. If all people go peacefully to their death, why would he think he deserved a different fate? Where did he get the right to demand eternal life? The person or people who came up with all this could have come up with the notion of eternal life—if they had been so inclined—but, evidently, they hadn't been and now it was too late to lodge a complaint. All the deadlines had passed many centuries before, and there were no indications of a revision in the offing. That could mean, thought Mileta Micić, that the only thing left to him was to raise his head and walk calmly where all had gone before while the chimes were tolling for eternal repose. But that image gave him no comfort either. It was easy to imagine the funereal scene—people at the cemetery, the excavated grave, the gravediggers with perspiring brows, women in black, men with crooked ties, snot-nosed children—and feel a part of the quavering emotions, but then followed the question of what they would all be doing the next day. Not what he would be doing, because for him it was clear: he would be lying in his coffin, while all the others went on living at their regular rhythms, as if Mileta Micić had never existed. Injustice, whispered Mileta Micić though he couldn't say why his departure to the other world would be "injustice," and then it occurred to him that with his departure in fact the whole world would be departing, because didn't certain philosophers claim that the world is only an external image of our inner world? When we are gone, they said, then there is no world, there is nothing, you came from emptiness and to emptiness you return. But, is that the truth? Mileta Micić wondered, and how to test the validity of the statement? Because, if I am the one who is imagining the whole world, then I am imagining others who are, supposedly, imagining their worlds. No, no, and no, this whole story is overwrought, the world is either one, integral, or it does not exist at all. His departure changes nothing. The sun comes up in the east, sets in the west, it hides somewhere at night from the moon and the stars, and red clouds at night, if he remembered correctly, predicted windy weather with longer or shorter spells of precipitation, of which there wouldn't be much, two millimeters tops, but only one millimeter was enough to drown a person. And of course, if he is already dead, the depth of the water is of no consequence whatsoever to him, this needs to be said since there are always the curious types who, intentionally or otherwise, either way, examine everything and ask hundreds of pointless questions, despite that fact that there is only a small number of truly important questions that need answering, or at least need a stab at an answer, during a lifetime. Though, thought Mileta Micić, this, too, is an exaggeration, because if a person already knows his fate, then no question matters—except one which might change that fate. In other words, there is no point to worrying and despairing, because whatever he tries, whatever answer he finds, nothing will be changed by it. At the end of everything, after all the questions and answers, after all the words and procedures, after all the trying and giving up, the same thing always remains—old, creaking, icy death. Which means, thought Mileta Micić, that one should never go into death without a sweater, just as one always takes a sweater along in the summertime, at the seaside, when going for a walk, because sea air is fickle, chilly at first, then damp, hot for a spell, then refreshing.

No, no, and no, Mileta Micić fretted, the answer to his question is not hidden in a sweater. The secret of life or death cannot be intertwined with knitting, though, on the other hand, he had to admit that knitting had always seemed a mystical act to him, the creation of a tangled structure that a person pulled onto himself and so, probably, became an unwilling accessory to the person who knitted him the sweater. There, instead of thinking about how to evade death, he was thinking of patterns and techniques for knitting. Knitting or crocheting, wondered Mileta Micić, suddenly uncertain of which is the more complicated and magical: two crisscrossed needles which seem to spar, or the crochet hook which, like a dentist's tool that is always inflicting pain, is forever hooking loops it has made itself, as if it wants to snare itself once and for all? He thought about this for a long time, and then he decided to lie down. The day had already stretched on beyond all measure, which was Mileta Micić's fault, he had to admit, as was his stubborn refusal to find meaning in the absence of meaning, which had never been something those far wiser than he was had had in hand. He stared at his hands as if he might get an answer from them. However, the hands merely fidgeted in his lap and kept their silence. Only the right thumb, frozen, pointed upwards at the ceiling lamp, so Mileta Micić's gaze followed it up. The lamp was large, old-fashioned, and dusty. The bottom of the lowest glass globe was littered with dead bugs and moths, among them, visibly apart, was the black, desiccated shell of a cockroach. How did the cockroach get up there into the lamp globe, Mileta Micić wondered, what is this supposed to mean? Maybe the cockroach tried to get close to the light source, the terrifying glow that propelled even the boldest members of its kind into a race into shadow and darkness? Perhaps, in other words, it was looking for the same thing Mileta Micić was feverishly trying to discover. And all I have managed to learn, Mileta Micić sighed, is that I am not so different from a cockroach and that the same end surely awaits me. He stared at the dusty sediment of death on the bottom of the glass globe of the old-fashioned ceiling lamp, but there was nothing moving there, nothing offered unexpected hope, dust is only dust, just as death is always only death, and all that was left for him to do was to close his eyes, everything else would play out on its own, as it had so many times before, as it was doing here, this instant, now, when, any minute, there, now!

THE YEARS have taken their toll: I wake up at night more often, and then, bereft of sleep, I go to the bathroom, perch on the bathtub, and stare at my reflection in the mirror. I used to roam the house, I'd go from room to room, turn on the television, turn it off, open the fridge and eat, but since my son's friends have started staying over, I have condemned myself to staying in the bathroom. Balding, with a potbelly and legs streaked with veins, I couldn't bear encounters with those young, muscular bodies, tanned faces framed in a full head of hair, and gleaming teeth that shone in the semi-dark of the hall as we passed each other. The boys were always polite: when they saw the light on in the bathroom they'd use the other toilet, by the kitchen, and leave me to my insomnia and attempts at fishing for a remedy in the medicine cabinet.

But last night, just as I was standing, legs planted apart, over the toilet bowl, emptying my bladder, the bathroom door opened and a young woman I had never seen before appeared in the doorway. Her hair was tousled, her make-up slightly smudged, and she was wearing a large white T-shirt which reached to her knees and under which, I sensed, she had nothing on. Her eyes were half-closed as she stepped into the bathroom, as if still half-asleep, or, which I more readily believed, under the sway of a just-smoked joint, so that only after her second step did she realize someone else was there. She stopped, her eyes widened, and her right hand flew up to smooth her hair. Meanwhile, powerless to change anything, I kept right on urinating noisily, feeling a blush rising over my face. The young woman finally woke up, as was clearly visible on her face, and her gaze dropped to my member. I looked at it, too, then shook it carefully and tucked it back into my pajama bottoms. The pajamas were old, with holes in the crotch and armpits, but I hoped those would go unnoticed.

"Hey," said the girl, "nice equipment."

I wasn't sure what she was referring to. "What equipment," I asked, "where?"

"That," said the girl and waved at my belly, which was protected by Goofy and Mickey Mouse.

My pajamas had Disney characters all over them. I had been given them several years before by my wife: she went to the States as a Fulbright fellow, came back with the pajamas, then went there again. She said she was going for professional advancement, but never said what had to be advanced. She'd get in touch at odd intervals to ask after Dejan, our son, and whether her goldfish was still alive. She never asked after me, and she never exactly answered my question of when she'd be coming back. It's not time yet, she'd say, or she'd just chuckle and quietly hang up.

Meanwhile the young woman came right over and I had to step back. "Hey," she said, "I don't bite, no worries, all I want to do is what you were doing. I assume you don't stand guard all night by the toilet bowl?"

I moved aside to let her pass, but the bathroom suddenly shrank, became crowded, and her elbow brushed my belly. The girl hiked up her T-shirt and sat down on the toilet. I was right: she wasn't wearing anything underneath.

"I am Vedrana," said the girl while the stream of her urine spashed the water.

"I am Dejan's father," I answered.

"So I take it," said the girl, "that Dejan is the guy sleeping in the next room?"

"Yes," I said, "Dejan is my son."

"Good-looking guy," replied the young woman. "He said right away he only lived with his father." She tore off two sheets of toilet paper and wiped between her legs. "So what happened to his mother? Did she die?" She dropped the paper into the toilet bowl and stood up. She scratched her belly button before she dropped her T-shirt, and in that brief moment I could see that her pubic hair was shaved.

"She didn't die," I said, "she just lives far away from here.

"In Australia?" asked the young woman. "Or New Zealand?"

"America," I answered.

"America is not far away," said the girl, "especially New York."

"I don't know where she is," I answered. I could hear my voice quaver.

The young woman heard it, too. She came a little closer, reached over to touch a Goofy right over my heart. "She gave you these pajamas, didn't she?" She moved her finger to the right and stopped at my left nipple, where there was a Mickey Mouse. She ran her finger around it gently and I felt my member slowly swelling. "Don't you think," the young woman went on, "that you are a little big for Goofy and Mickey?"

I grabbed her by the wrist and pushed her hand away. "There are those," I said, "who never grow up."

Then the door to the bathroom opened and there was Dejan. He, too, was wearing a large white T-shirt, his hair was tousled, his eyes bloodshot and his lips chapped. "What's going on here," he asked, "can't a person get any sleep in this house?" He looked at me, then at the young woman, and then he looked down at my erect member which made Goofy and Mickey Mouse look like images in a warped mirror. "What is the world coming to," he said, "a father steals a girl from his son. Does that make any sense? And you," he looked at the young woman, "what is your name again?"

"Vedrana," said the girl.

"It's not her fault," I barged in. "I was in the bathroom when she came in, and we spent a few minutes in conversation. Nothing happened," I finished, evading Dejan's gaze.

"Nothing is ever going to happen to a person who wears pajamas like those," said Dejan. He inspected me from head to toe. "You're missing Donald Duck," he concluded. "Did you notice," he turned to the young woman, "there's no Donald Duck?"

"If there is someone missing," said the young woman, "it's Duckie."

I looked at her and she winked back.

"You two are thick as thieves," said Dejan, "should I go?"

"You stay," said the young woman, "I am going." She patted my face. "Look after the equipment," she said, "Duckie will be back one of these days."

"My room is the one on the right," said Dejan after her, "don't be going the wrong way. Excuse me," he turned to me, "I've got to pee."

"Sure," I said, "that's what everyone does here."

While he was moving past me he brushed my stomach with his

DAVID ALBAHARI

elbow in the same place the girl had. Unlike her, he didn't want me to watch him urinate, so he stood sideways to the toilet bowl. He urinated long and loud, and as far as I could tell he, too, had nothing on under the white T-shirt. When he'd finished, he looked in the mirror, bared his teeth, licked his lips. "Hell," he said when our eyes met, "if this were any other girl you could have her, but she's one snarky snake woman and I'm not finished with her yet. What did she say her name was?"

"Vedrana," I said.

"Vedrana," he repeated. "Nice name."

I said nothing.

Dejan shot me a thoughtful glance. "Is it that you dislike her," he asked, "or are you angry at me about something?"

"Why would I be angry at you?"

He shrugged. "Dunno," he said, "aren't fathers and sons supposed to be bickering all the time?"

"We never fight," I answered.

"Maybe that's what we're doing wrong," Dejan went on, "maybe we should be harder on each other." He came closer and inspected me from head to toe again. "She's right," he said, "no Donald Duck."

"So what now," I asked, "should I throw these pajamas out?"

"You've been wearing them for six years," he said, "maybe the time really has come for them to go into the trash."

The two of us fell silent. I don't know what Dejan was thinking, but I was imagining my pajamas in the trash can, and then I saw the garbage men picking them up and shaking them out, and how one of them slipped his middle finger out through the hole in the crotch. I could clearly see the finger wiggling forward and back, like a worm, while the other garbage men snickered.

"Well, then," said Dejan, "off I go."

"I'll stay here a while longer," I said.

Dejan raised his right hand in parting, smiled, and left. He came right back. "I forgot to tell you," he said, "Mom called last night."

"What did she say?"

"Nothing."

"She can't have said nothing."

/174

Dejan thought for a minute. "No," he said, "she didn't say anything."

Nothing is nothing, there was no point in insisting on this any further. Dejan left, I perched on my old spot on the bathtub and stared at my face in the mirror. Then I got up, stripped off the pajamas and dropped them into the waste basket. I didn't know whether I felt any better, all I knew was that I was colder. Loud laughter could be heard from Dejan's room, and later, when I was back in my own room, I heard how his bed was creaking in the regular rhythm of intercourse. I ought to put something on, I thought, but I couldn't think of a single item of clothing. I closed my eyes, clenched my fists, and gave myself over to the cold that climbed up my legs, I stood there waiting for silence to reign in the house.

No, THE SPIRITS will never rest as far as Ilija is concerned. For some he is mainly an eminent writer, but for others, and there are more and more of these, he is one thing only, a traitor to his country. At the funeral, Veljko, Ilija's neighbor, was thinking, How strange that in one case it's acceptable to forgive and forget what were truly reprehensible actions, while for someone like Ilija there is no erasing a blot even though no one can remember precisely how it came about. Even Ilija was no longer sure what he was being blamed for, but he bowed his head, all those years, and resigned himself to suffering with the burden of the affront.

An outrage, thought Veljko, a real outrage, and he's such a fine man. A woman standing in front of him turned around and shot him a quizzical glance. Ah, he must have been thinking out loud again, Veljko frowned, realizing he should be more watchful, turned and headed toward the cemetery exit. And besides, he had used the wrong verb tense: Ilija had *been* a fine man, but he no longer was nor would he ever be again. Veljko sighed. Now there was nothing to do but accustom himself to Ilija's absence. But he sensed that this was not going to be easy, especially since over the last years, as his illness progressed, Ilija had come by more often. He had been stopping by daily over the last six or seven months, at all different times, sometimes in early morning, or in the afternoon, or, often, in the evening, and once or twice he woke Veljko in the middle of the night, though then he'd stay for only ten minutes and not say a word.

Veljko never had anything against Ilija's behavior. Writers can be extravagant and it is silly to expect any sort of explanation. Ilija tried to say something about it several times, but Veljko interrupted him right away and told him to save his words for his next heroic deed of the pen.

"No, no," Ilija would protest, "they are not deeds, they're misdeeds, believe me."

Veljko, of course, did not believe him, because every reader, even those with the worst of intentions, had to admit that one could feel the spirit of wisdom and greatness in his every sentence. In terms of his creative prowess, no one could say a word against him, friend or foe. Indeed, his foes never spoke of what Ilija wrote or accomplished; they spoke only of what Ilija *had not* done. Veljko could even rattle off a list of the main gripes because they squawked them like parrots at every available opportunity. Even when the news of Ilija's death was made public and many of those who valued his work had only the most laudatory things to say, his foes were waving around posters with anti-Ilija slogans.

Had they brought the posters to the funeral, Veljko would certainly have assaulted them, nothing would have stopped him. The dead must be respected, at least while they are still with us. Once they had departed for their world, that was something else again, in Veljko's opinion, and he was not particularly upset when he saw a large poster with Ilija's picture and the words "Ilija is a disgrace to his nation" on a wall by the cemetery entrance.

The poster did upset a young woman in black who set to ripping it off the wall. At first she tore it slowly, in long strips, then she ripped off pieces of it faster and faster, stomping on the shreds, and finally she burst into frantic tears and hammered the crumbling wall with her fists.

Veljko, who had been playing the role of indifferent bystander up to that point, could no longer hold himself back. He went over to the young woman and tried taking her by the hand, repeating over and over again, "OK, it's OK, just take it easy, everything will be all right." No part of the sentence was true, but nothing else occurred to him to say. Sometimes lies are a help and Veljko felt the young woman's defiance weaken. The frantic sobs also subsided, which gave Veljko a chance to pass her a tissue and flash her a smile of encouragement. Then he leaned over a bit and said to her, nearly in her ear, that Ilija must have been her very favorite writer when she was grieving so deeply for him.

The young woman pulled away from him, and answered, "Favorite writer? Not at all, he was my father."

Veljko stepped back—he knew Ilija had gotten a divorce many years before, but it never occurred to him that the man might have had children. He took a better look at the woman's face from a safe distance. The longer he looked, the more he saw she was not lying. The lines of her face fit the lines of Ilija's face without a doubt, and her nose was a smaller version of his. Her smile, too. Only her eyes were different. Ilija had had dark eyes and a piercing, often unpleasant, gaze, while her eyes were a pliant blue, probably, thought Veljko, coming from her mother's side.

Now those blue eyes stared at him and Veljko hastened to introduce himself. He said that he was a friend of her father's and that they had become particularly close over the last six or seven months, during a time, as he said, when Ilija was stopping by his place every day.

"Oh," said the young woman, "then I know who you are. You are Veljko, right? Dad spoke of you. You used to have a dog until recently, and now you have goldfish." She smiled and again fixed her gaze on Veljko.

First he thought of the dog he had spent the past fifteen years with and had recently had put down at the vet's, and he could barely stem the tears. Then he thought of the goldfish, Hiromi and Yoko, as he called them, and a third one, nameless, and then he looked up and said boldly, "Would you like to see them? I live nearby, as you obviously know."

The young woman nodded, came over and slipped her arm through his. They set off just as the people attending the funeral were starting to disperse and Veljko picked up the pace a little. He wasn't eager to run into anyone he knew, especially now that Ilija's daughter, whom no one, he sensed, was aware of, had taken him by the arm and perhaps even rested her lower arm on his hip. He glanced stealthily to the right and met her gaze. They smiled and Ilija asked what her name was.

"Samba," said the young woman.

Veljko thought perhaps he hadn't heard correctly. "What do you mean—samba," he asked, "samba, you mean like the rumba, the dance?"

"Yes," said the young woman, "except the samba is not the rumba."

"Still," said Veljko, "I have never heard of Samba as a name."

"There is a first time for everything," said the young woman and laughed aloud.

"There is a first time for everything," repeated Veljko, "Ilija has a story with that for its title and there's a young woman in it with that same ringing laugh."

"Never read It myself," said the young woman. Then she sighed and said, "I am not a big literature fan." This sounded like something she was weary of repeating and she'd rather talk about something else.

"We're almost there," said Veljko.

"I can hardly wait to see the goldfish," said the young woman.

And sure enough, as soon as they entered Veljko's apartment she went straight to the aquarium and didn't move away from it even when Vejlko came back with a bottle of brandy and two glasses. "It is right for us have a drink for his soul." He handed a full glass to the young woman and she downed it in a single swig, never looking away from the goldfish. Then she asked Veljko, "Do you have any idea why no one likes him?"

"Who?" asked Veljko.

"My father," said the young woman. She dipped a fingertip into the water and tried to lure the fish with it.

I need another drink, thought Veljko and said, "He was better and different from them, and here no one can be forgiven for that."

She said nothing but he knew she didn't believe him.

"Samba," he called to her in a soft voice, and when she looked up, her eyes brimming with tears, he said, "goldfish are actually little carp. Did you know that?"

"No," said Samba, "I didn't." And she turned slowly to face him.

THOUGH HE had heeded his inner voice and gone to Belgrade, Hinko still wasn't able to figure out what he was actually doing there. He had gotten by for nearly fifty years without going to the land of his parents, and considering how little he liked Belgrade, he was sorry now that he had reneged on his promise. He'd made the promise to himself the day he first heard about what his father endured in the Yugoslav prisons and camps after World War II, after which he had been forced to sign away all of his property and go to Israel. There he met Dina Wolf, from a prominent Zagreb Jewish family; they married and late in 1961, after many tries, they had a son, Hinko. Some twenty years later Hinko was alone. First his father died, suffering from ailments he had picked up, Hinko believed, when he was interned at the Goli Otok camp, and two months later his mother passed, stricken by grief at Hinko's father, Šmuel's, untimely death…

There was only so much grief Hinko could process. The death of one parent is often a crushing blow, but if the death of the other follows immediately after it, this second death is not as hard. The tear ducts have no relief left to offer most mourners, and it all begins to seem like the prelude to a farce. So the death of a second parent is more quickly and easily taken in stride, while that first loss always lingers, even when we think we are done with it.

Whatever the case, after their deaths, Hinko felt a sudden surge of freedom. His parents had never held him back, indeed they were always urging him on to one thing after another, and it was precisely in this respect that Hinko felt the tug of freedom, for now he could give in to his favorite state—yes, simply put, doing nothing at all. While his parents were alive, Hinko hadn't dared to stop. As soon as they'd see him lounging in a café or enjoying music (only classical!), they would cook something up for him to do: language lessons (by now he had attended courses in Spanish, Russian, French and Esperanto) or classes in the martial arts and yoga (tai chi, meditation and Jiu-Jitsu). In Israel, where the ideology of strenuous exertion, a brutal absurdity dating from the time of the Jewish Zionist pioneers, had blossomed into a commando mindset, the usual slackers and good-for-nothings were regarded with biting scorn, which meant that Hinko had little to hope for in terms of respect there. Hence Belgrade suddenly occurred to him and he took an interest. If Israeli society would have nothing to do with him, he would have nothing to do with it. He'd go somewhere else, he was determined. But where? He pondered this and then he thought of Belgrade though another twenty years would pass before he finally decided to give it a try.

Despite all they had been through in Yugoslavia, Hinko's parents never stopped talking about the mystical beauty of Belgrade, the great cafés, the exciting music, mysterious Kalemegdan, so it was quite natural for Hinko to decide that the time had come to get to know his background, and meet some of the remaining family members who were living in Belgrade and Subotica. His mother's relatives were in Zagreb, but these days that was in a different country, Croatia, where Hinko had not been prepared to go, though he loved the sea and many Israeli friends had given him glowing reports of the beauty of the Croatian islands.

Now he had begun thinking he ought to go to Croatia and find an oasis of peace on one of those islands. Belgrade wasn't working for him, that much was clear soon after he got there. He stayed at the Mosvka hotel in the center of town, convinced that this would be the best place for him to get a feel for the real rhythm of the city. The rhythm, he soon learned, was fascinating but it reminded him a little of the hurly-burly around the main bus station in Tel Aviv and this was a strike against Belgrade. Hinko did not like noise, a natural preference for a person who was happiest doing nothing. He didn't find the cafés congenial, and he was especially put off by the ones where singers performed songs that had the same cadence and histrionics they had in Israel. Kalemegdan was indeed mysterious, but he was alarmed by the large zoo there. Hinko belonged to one of those organizations that fought to sustain nature and they felt that zoos were the pinnacle of human hypocrisy. If he had had at least two or three people with him, Hinko would have begun marching up and down in front of the entrance to the zoo. In his tentative Serbian he even cobbled together the slogan, "Better Dead than Zooed."

The only thing he had no complaints about was the food. The cuisine reminded him of the food he had eaten in his family home in Jerusalem, but this was much tastier. Hinko figured his mother must have forgotten the recipes from her native land, and then he chose not to dwell on that and gave himself over to the moussakas, oven-baked beans, prosciutto and cheese, beef stew, grilled cutlets and sausages. He was not observant so he had no worries about keeping kosher, though every time he bit into a piece of bacon he felt a twinge of guilt. Maybe that is what contributed, as a sort of negative counter-weight, to the accumulation of so much dislike for Belgrade. Everything irked him, the little beggars who came into the cafés and pestered the guests, the unbearable throngs in the walkway under the Zeleni Venac open market which totally spoiled the appeal of the market, the warlike cries of young men and boys who traveled in packs like gangs of delinquents; the overflowing, foul-smelling garbage containers, the men who hosed down the streets at night who shouted as if it were noon, the trash strewn all over the sidewalks, the scowling men and disgruntled women on their way home from work who clearly reviled everything around them.

Despite this, Hinko could not bring himself to go back to Israel. One of the reasons for his lack of decisiveness arose after he visited the Jewish cemetery in Belgrade. Hinko knew his father's family had numbered many people before World War II, but he did not expect to see so many tombstones of his relatives. There wasn't a single one, however, on which he saw the name Hinko. Where had his name come from? His father once told him that the boy's mother had insisted on the name, and when Hinko asked her that straight out, she stopped, measured him with a sad glance, and then dismissed the question with a shrug. "There is something I didn't want to forget," and when Hinko asked her what she hadn't meant to forget, she merely put her finger to her lips, turned, and left.

Hinko didn't like secrets, though this story about his name did not sound like such a big secret. If his mother didn't want to lose or forget the name, that could mean only one thing: that at some point in her life there had been a person whose name had been Hinko, and that he, being given the name, had become a symbol of a fate he knew nothing about. He felt this was mean to his father, who surely knew all about it. Every time his father heard the name, thought Hinko, he must have felt a pang in his heart, his chest, somewhere. He couldn't understand what sort of game his parents were playing, especially since by all accounts their relationship had been harmonious. He therefore wanted to find out who the first Hinko was, the proto-Hinko, so to speak. Where was the name from, he wondered, it certainly wasn't originally Jewish, regardless of the fact that many Jewish children living in Vojvodina and Slavonia were named that, as he found by reading several books on the history of Jewish communities in Central Europe.

This offered him no consolation. Perhaps his resistance to Belgrade would have been less if the story about the name Hinko hadn't gotten tangled up in everything, giving Hinko a constant bitter aftertaste. Led by the bitter taste, Hinko was always coming up with new complaints about the city buses, the overcrowded restaurants and cafés, the expensive stores, the ruthless drivers and even more ruthless traffic cops. He could rant about all this for hours, with an agitation and fervor typical of Israelis, until someone, in a more or less abrupt tone, warned him to shut up.

"What is it with you Israelis?" asked a young woman cautiously at the synagogue. "You act like everyone is against you, and then, when you are attacked and criticized, you immediately clutch at Zionism and start leveling accusations for every word spoken."

"Really?" Hinko was surprised, though he had long had a sneaking feeling that this might be true.

The young woman went on, "There in Israel, you lose the knack for how to carry on a true dialogue," she said, "because everyone starts shouting immediately and they don't let the people they are speaking with get a word in edgewise."

"That isn't real dialogue? Aren't the shouting and the noise what real conversation is all about?" asked Hinko in an attempt to extend an olive branch.

But the young woman just looked at him a while longer and then muttering something which, in her clumsy English, sounded to Hinko like, "You Israelis are all the same," she smiled and left.

Later when he went back to the hotel, he remembered something else and called the young woman. "Hi," he said when she picked up, "I was thinking about our conversation and I see you are right. It is true that we in Israel have almost lost the skill of having a real conversation, a true exchange, but much worse than the shouting and the noise is that many people think monolog is, in fact, conversation." He stopped talking and waited, out of breath, to hear what the young woman from the synagogue would say to that, and then she coughed and asked, "Who gave you my phone number?"

"I got it at the synagogue," said Hinko, "right after the service."

"The Rabbi gave you my phone number?" the young woman asked, incredulous.

"The Rabbi's wife," said Hinko. She was from Israel, and she seemed so eager to have the chance to talk with someone in Hebrew that she couldn't stop. They talked about all sorts of things, and during a brief pause Hinko asked her a few questions about the young woman from the synagogue. It turned out that the Rabbi's wife knew her well, or rather, as she said, all the members of such a small community knew each other well. She urged Hinko to get in touch with the woman and even gave him her phone number scribbled on an empty cigarette pack.

"The Rabbi's wife gave you my phone number?" repeated the young woman, still incredulous.

Hinko was confused. To be so surprised that someone would give someone else a phone number was really odd; he could have gotten the number in several different ways, through the post office, for instance, or at the Jewish community office. He couldn't understand the young woman's reaction, but he was sure something was wrong. "If you'd rather we don't talk," he said, finally, "that's not a problem. I will hang up right now," which he did, without waiting for her answer. And when the phone rang a few moments later in his hotel room he did not pick it up.

The next day waiting for him at the concierge's desk was a message from the young woman, "Call me." The words were written above her name—Esther—while under it, as an afterthought, were the words "Thank you." Hinko called her right away and, before she could say anything he apologized for his rudeness. Esther said she was the one who should be apologizing, with which Hinko immediately disagreed, and so they wrangled pointlessly for a time, until Esther said that she had had it with all this thrashing of straw.

"My mother used to say that," said Hinko, "after every broadcast of a session of the Israeli parliament, she'd say in a hoarse voice, 'Those idiots are just thrashing straw.'"

Esther said she'd be glad to go on talking with him about the thrashing of straw, or anything else for that matter, if Hinko were up for meeting with her later that afternoon or evening. She didn't live far from the hotel where he was staying, she said. Why didn't he stop by her place, so they could figure out where they'd go from there.

Hinko looked at his watch. There was still plenty of time for him to get to the open market and taste the cheese sold by the lively village women, and then have a cup of coffee at one of the restaurants in the pedestrian zone, and then spruce up for his visit to Esther. At the open market, surrounded by the smells of the different things for sale, he spent a long time trying to decide whether to buy Esther some flowers, and finally, as he had many times before, he chose not to. He simply was not a flowers kind of a guy. He said as much to Esther when she opened the door of her little apartment on Strahinjića Bana Street. "That's OK," Esther reassured him. "But do tell, what else are you not?" Hinko looked at her, baffled, and said he didn't know what she meant.

"Well just a moment ago you said you are not a flowers kind of a guy," answered Esther. "I am interested in what else you are not for if I find out now, it will be easier for me later on. Tell me, for instance, do you dance?"

No, Hinko was not a dancing kind of a guy, just as he was not a fighting kind of a guy, and not the kind of guy who spoke about his feelings out loud. "I am a simple man," he defended himself, but he sensed this no longer held water. In fact, he was beginning to feel that he had been in Belgrade long enough by then that this was changing. One can stay unchanged in a city only so long. After that the defense mechanisms of the personality lose their grip and the new situations begin to exert an influence. A person changes and becomes, if not somebody else, then a new version of his old self, which can be as different from who he used to be as the sky is from the earth. But ever since he had gotten to know Esther something changed inside him and it was as if he had become indifferent, or at least more indifferent, to the things that used to bother him. He even stopped protesting when they served him warm beer at cafés, which had earlier sent him into a seething fury. This time it happened in the garden of a café not far from the place where Esther lived. She ordered a lemonade and Hinko ordered a dark beer and Esther noticed the wince of distaste when he had taken the first sip. She asked him what was wrong, and at first he avoided answering, but finally he told her what was bothering him.

"Then why drink it?" she hissed at him. "Why not ask them to bring you another one?"

Even if he'd wanted to answer, Hinko wouldn't have known what to say. He had caught himself thinking that maybe it didn't matter so much when the men hosing down the street got your shoes, pants, or sneakers wet, just as he realized that garbage smells the same everywhere and it would be impossible for them to empty all the containers at exactly the same time. He was realizing that all of this was only a part of life, a part that had its role in a larger picture, but he made no effort to take in the bigger picture.

"Why aren't you saying anything?" Esther whispered angrily. "Say something!"

"What should I say?" whispered Hinko, hoping they weren't attracting too much attention.

"Anything," Esther prodded him, "don't be scared!"

"Why would I be scared?" answered Hinko, and probably to confirm those words he suddenly straightened up and thrust out his chest. Confidence, he thought, now that is what I need.

Confidence, thought Esther, now that is what he needs.

So, without realizing it, they were both thinking the same words. Then Hinko thought he would be even more confident if only he could change his name—to Aaron, for instance, or Moshe. Anything but Hinko. Who was Hinko anyway, he said to himself huffily, who was it his mother was so intent on remembering that she named her son after him? Out of the corner of his eye he watched Esther tapping her fingertips on the surface of the table. Judging by the speed of the rhythm she was tapping she was still angry but he mustered the courage to ask her whether she had ever met anyone named Hinko besides him.

"Never," answered Esther, looked at him and said, "You are my first Hinko!" which she apparently liked because she went on repeating it, "My first Hinko, my first Hinko..." As she was ordering she even said to the waitress, "Another lemonade for me, and one more dark beer, but a cold one this time, for him." She pointed at Hinko as if he were sitting in the next restaurant over and not at the same table. "That's my Hinko," Esther said and winked at the waitress.

The waitress shrugged and answered, "Never heard it before myself."

"I'm telling you," said Esther to Hinko as the waitress walked away, "no one has ever heard of—" She suddenly stopped and struck her forehead, "What am I thinking, my best friend's father's name is Hinko! How could I forget!"

"Is he Jewish?" Hinko asked carefully.

"Of course. His name was Hinko Klajn, Dr. Hinko Klajn."

"His name was," repeated Hinko, "meaning he died?"

"No," Esther shook her head, "but he had to change his name, poor man. Now he is Ariel. Ariel Katan."

"Why?"

Esther sighed. "It's a long story," she said finally. "I don't feel like going into it."

"Don't tell the whole thing," Hinko advised her, "the end is what matters most in any story."

The waitress stopped by their table again, set down the beer and lemonade, and waited for Hinko to pay. "Enjoy," she said and disappeared.

"So?" Hinko asked Esther.

"I don't know if I'll be able to sum it up it well, but it looks as if my best friend's father, before he met her mother, had a passionate fling with a Jewish woman from Zagreb whom he met on a work camp team or during the corn harvest. Flings usually don't last long but this one turned into a nightmare, at least as far as my best friend's father was concerned. His passion was soon spent, as it is for most men, but the woman simply would not or could not accept it. She wrote him letters, sent messages, took pictures of them, arrived with no warning in the middle of the night and banged on the door, waking up all the neighbors."

"And then she moved to Israel?" Hinko interrupted her.

Esther looked at him, surprised, and asked, "How did you know?"

"It's a long story," said Hinko. "Maybe I'll tell you some day. So what happened with your friend's parents?"

"One day the woman announced to my friend's future father that she was pregnant and that he, as father of the child, was responsible to look after it. Hinko Klajn had just graduated from Medical School and wasted no time quarreling. He packed up his things and, by way of Italy and France, he got to America where, desiring to make a new beginning in his life, he changed his name to Ariel Katan... Many years later my best friend came across some yellowed documents quite by chance when going through the drawers of her father's old desk, from which she learned that the name Ariel Katan masked the name Hinko Klajn."

"So is he still in America?"

"No," said Esther. "After his wife's death he sank gradually into the void of Alzheimer's disease and my friend decided to bring him to Belgrade. She had moved back to Belgrade some ten years earlier and could no longer bear those grueling transatlantic flights. It was simpler for her to bring her father here and place him in one of the new, private homes for the elderly and infirm.

"So where is he now?" asked Hinko.

"At the Voždovac Home for the Elderly. I can give you the address if you're interested, though I cannot imagine why this story has gotten you so worked up?" Esther looked at him thoughtfully, like a true hunter. And she only relaxed when he promised to tell her everything the next time they went out.

The next morning at about ten o'clock, Hinko was at the entrance to the Home. When he said who he was there to see, the young woman at the front desk asked him whether he was aware of

Mr. Katan's condition. Hinko said that he knew, and she told him the room number in a soft voice as if giving him the secret code for opening a safe full of precious things. When he got to the room, however, he found a cleaning lady there who dispatched him to the back garden. "While the weather is nice," she told him, "he's better off sitting in the garden, in the shade, with the birds chirping." She pointed Hinko to the corridor that led to the yard and asked him, "Are you a relative?" Hinko just waved and took off down the corridor. He got to the glass door and through it saw a large yard in which there were several elderly people. Only one was sitting in the shade in a wheelchair and he concluded that this must be Mr. Katan. He opened the door, stepped out into the yard and walked decisively over to him. Mr. Katan was dozing and when he stopped in front of him, Hinko could clearly see a thin thread of spittle drooling out of the side of his mouth. He took a tissue from his pocket, leaned over and wiped his chin. As he was doing this, Mr. Katan opened his eyes and clutched at Hinko's hand. His gaze was full of fear, but then, slowly, quite slowly, something different appeared in his eyes, something that Hinko took to be recognition, especially when the old man grinned and drew him closer, so that Hinko had to kneel and lean his head on the man's chest. He didn't know what Mr. Katan could have seen in his face, perhaps his mother's features, but whatever it was the old man wasn't letting go. He hugged him, patted his head, and Hinko made no move to pull away. His face thrust into the old man's clothes, he breathed deeply the familiar scent of old people which one can smell nowhere else, because it is coming from the other side, where everything, after all, is different.